What Protects Our Heritage
and
Other Aberrations

I've been a fan of Mist's vampire series and was really excited to check out her short story collection. She did not disappoint. These stories are mean as hell and brilliant, and they bring Icelandic folklore to life in the grisliest way possible. Every story in here is killer, but the novelette that closes out the collection is definitely a standout.

—Elford Alley, author of *High Strangeness* and *The Corpse Walker*

What Protects Our Heritage and Other Aberrations

Villimey Mist

Brigids Gate Press

Edited by S.D. Vassallo

Formatted by Stephanie Ellis

Cover illustration and design by Kristina Osborn

First Edition: November 2024

ISBN (paperback): 978-1-963355-18-5
ISBN (ebook): 978-1-963355-17-8
Library of Congress Control Number: 2024947518

BRIGIDS GATE PRESS

Overland Park, Kansas

www.brigidsgatepress.com

Printed in the United States of America

To my late grandfather, Hafsteinn, an adventurous soul who loved storytelling of all kinds.

Contents

INTRODUCTION

BY KEV HARRISON

Mention the name Villimey Mist in most horror reader circles and people will immediately bring up her hit 'Nocturnal' series of vampire novels, beginning with 2018's *Nocturnal Blood*. And rightly so, with Leia Walker's vampiric adventures selling in huge numbers and spawning three sequels to date.

Here, though, in *What Protects Our Heritage and Other Aberrations*, Mist shows the broad range of her writing talents. The subject matter and tone of the stories differs wildly, from the playful and even humorous to the deeply melancholic, and the downright terrifying. Yes, there is one vampire story here (more on that later), but zooming in on the title of this collection and its twin themes of heritage and aberration provides the reader with a glimpse of what to expect, rather than simply being a catchy moniker.

Heritage, of course, comes in the form of Mist's own provenance on the volcanic island of Iceland. In this collection, and indeed throughout Mist's career to date, we see more and more of the unique folklore and legend which this storied country of frigid cold and burning magma has to offer. Beginning with the opening tale, 'The Girl with the Hooves,' the reader is thrust into the unforgiving landscape in a tale with immense emotional weight to match its bite. While in 'They Came from the Rocks,' a story told found-footage style, via emails about an excavation project, we find another of Iceland's mythic monsters.

The next Icelandic encounter is in 'Hell of a Ride,' this time placing outsiders in harm's way on the island, once again with wonderfully evocative use of an entity from native folklore. Next, 'The Hag's Gift' flips that situation and places the titular hag, an Icelandic witch, no less, abroad, and things only turn more ghastly from there.

Finally, we have 'The Yule Lads are Coming,' an ode to the nation's forebears of Christmas, packed with vengeful violence, and the titular novelette, 'What Protects Out Heritage: An Icelandic Cryptid Story,' which is part tribute to the bravery of the Icelandic rescue service and part cautionary tale about wild places, wild things and treading into the unknown at the extremes of the earth.

Dotted among these Icelandic tales are others, beginning with 'Survival of the Fittest,' the only vampire story of this collection and one which places the blood drinker into an imaginative, unfamiliar scenario and one I've never seen or thought about before. This is closely followed by 'Tupperware Party,' a delightfully furious and frenetic revenge tale; 'All You Can Drink Buffet,' which skilfully weaves commentary on Japanese work culture with disturbing horror imagery which will live rent free in the reader's mind forever. Finally, 'The Perfect Time' provides a unique, disturbing take on the post-apocalyptic, with not a zombie in sight.

And so, to the second part of the title, and 'aberrations.' A theme we see throughout this collection is the outsider, struggling to survive and find their way in various incarnations of a cruel world. From the opening story's girl with the hooves, through the vampire and her opposite number, to the woman who has lost everything and who is just trying to recover on an Icelandic holiday, we find a cast of outsiders throughout this collection, with each one interpreting their own sense of loss, displacement, or whatever it may be with instincts which feel unique to them, as well as real, and believable.

All this points to the growing strength and confidence of the writer who, as with the mixtapes of my generation or the playlists of today's, has spliced together these tales into a composite whole which provides the full metaphorical rollercoaster of emotions, from sorrow to hilarity, disgust, and more besides.

I invite you to enjoy this compendium of stories and, like me, to eagerly await the aberrations still to come.

The Girl with the Hooves

The mountains of Iceland cried when I was born.

My grandmother used to say that often whenever she gazed upon me. A landslide hit my parents' house one winter night and crushed them. When my grandparents cleared the rubble, the only warm body they found was me, cradled in my mother's arms. I was the reason she died when giving birth. I was the deadly price she paid to bring a child into this frigid world. Nevertheless, my grandparents took me in and raised me instead of Mother and Father.

As I grew older, my grandparents quickly realized I was different from the other kids in our tiny village. My teeth were sharper than the average child's; no wet nurse allowed me near their breasts, and I was fed cow's milk instead.

"It fits a child like you," my grandmother said, as she gave me the last drops from the old cow's teat in a chipped, wooden bowl.

My ears were elongated like a rabbit's, so my grandparents forced me to sleep with the livestock. The sheep didn't mind my presence and their wool kept me warm during the long winter nights.

"Of course they don't mind it. You're more like them than us," Grandmother spat one morning, and glared at the tiny knobs protruding from my forehead. However, her loathing was directed most at my feet.

Instead of human feet, I was born with hooves.

To my family, I was more animal than human. To the world, I was a monster.

At first, people, mostly adults, avoided me like I was beset with yellow, pulsing pustules. Then when they saw I was harmless, the village kids began their torture. It started with poking my legs with sticks when I turned my back at them. Then it escalated to throwing rocks while they hid behind fish sheds.

"Devil child, Devil child!" they jeered every time.

The adults did nothing, some of them even encouraged the kids by telling them to leave me in the middle of a frozen pond, knowing I would have a hard time walking on the ice with my hooves. They succeeded on multiple occasions because I had no way of defending myself.

"Why do the kids call me Devil child, Grandmother?" I asked, holding back my tears because my sobs annoyed my grandfather.

Busy with mixing sheep's blood, the innards of sheep, and oats together to make slátur, Grandmother barely spared me a glance. "Because your mother slept with the Devil. Simple as that."

I turned to Grandfather, who was stitching the slátur and putting them in the boiling pot. "Is that why all the kids are being so mean to me, even when I haven't done anything to them?" I asked.

Grandfather avoided my intense gaze and focused on the stitching. He rarely spoke to me.

Grandmother shoved me aside with a scoff. "Yes, but you're also bad luck. Always have been."

Maybe she was right. It would explain the odd occurrences that would befall us every now and then. Like how some of the sheep disappeared when they were grazing near the mountains. The shepherds discovered their mutilated remains days later. The sensible people in the village chalked it up to ferocious foxes and minks. The superstitious ones all pointed their fingers at me.

Our misfortunes got worse over time. The weather turned bad come autumn. Sleets and hails ruined our little harvest. Some of our livestock became ill, and Grandfather was forced to slaughter them all and burn the carcasses. The stench of burning wool and animal hide stuck to our clothes till winter came. Nobody would buy or trade with us, not even when I hid in the house. Food became scarce, and my grandparents turned their frustrations on me. It was usually Grandmother who struck me with her cane. Grandfather only watched, a mixture of pitiful loathing shining in his droopy eyes.

I endured it. After all, I had no one but them.

In the end, my grandparents had no other option than to move across the country. Where the grass was supposedly greener. What little we had from our humble abode was packed in a small carriage.

Grandmother gave my grandfather a hard, meaningful look before lumbering up onto the wagon. She thrust her open palm at me when I attempted to climb as well. "Not you. You have to go with your grandfather to pick mountain thyme."

Grandfather shuddered when he took my hand. It didn't stem from the cold winter gale. Gathering the herbs must have been an important task to him to ignore his repulsion of me.

I looked behind my shoulder. Grandmother didn't see us off. Didn't even wave as she stared ahead. A knot wrapped itself around my insides. Sadness lingered in my heart. Why did I think that a goodbye would matter to her?

Mountain thyme grew all over the country and I spotted a few tiny bushes as we ascended the peak. "I see some thyme over there, Grandfather."

Grandfather glanced behind his shoulder but said nothing. Just pulled me along, ignoring the patches of herb near us.

We stumbled over the little rocks that littered the steep and treacherous terrain. The sharp ones scraped through the furs of my hooves. Wincing, out of breath, and drenched in sweat, I begged Grandfather to let us take a break.

He ignored my pleas, gripped my hand tighter and continued our trek.

We had been hiking for what felt like hours, the carriage no smaller than a rock from our view. The herbs we'd been tasked to gather didn't seem to grow that high up the mountain. My throat was parched but Grandfather wouldn't allow me a sip of water. He'd be too afraid my tongue would poison it.

Suddenly, he stopped. I staggered into him with a small yelp. Big boulders littered the path, big enough for a large person to hide. Snow covered the ground. No mountain thyme in sight.

"Why have we stopped, Grandfather?" I asked as I wrapped the thin scarf around my neck, shivering. The air was colder and thinner this high up the mountain. My hooves wobbled from fatigue.

Grandfather's gaze shifted upwards. "God forgive me for what I'm about to do," he said with a croak.

I cocked my head to the side, unsure if he was directing his speech at me or towards the blackened sky. Was he disappointed there were no herbs here? If that was the reason, we could just turn back and pick the ones I saw at the beginning of our trek. I reached out, ready to pull on his coarse coat.

His hands shot forwards and clutched my throat.

I gasped and faltered backwards, bulging eyes staring in disbelief at the man I had thought cared for me in some way. I clawed at his arms, bursts of panicked air escaping my lips. "Please, don't."

"You've brought nothing but sorrow and misfortune to our family. We should have done this a long time ago. We should have left you in the rubble with your whore of a mother!" Grandfather grunted, applying more pressure against my windpipe.

My eyes watered and, for a moment, Grandfather's blurry shape disappeared from my vision. His hold of me slackened, then released. Perhaps he regretted his decision? I coughed and hacked, blinking back tears that came unbidden. When my heart slowed its thrashing in my ears, I heard screams.

Grandfather's screams.

The earth rumbled. Something big moved slowly in my peripheral vision.

I froze. Despite the burning in my throat, I clasped my hands on my mouth.

Grandfather sprinted, screaming bloody murder as he descended the mountain. I'd never heard him so afraid. Not even when he was near me.

The big boulder on his left *rose up*, arms shooting out, and grabbed him. A giant figure in mossy clothing held him in its hand.

Grandfather kept sobbing and pleading. The figure's massive head glanced at me before turning back at Grandfather. Its other arm reached forth and held Grandfather's midsection. In one, quick twist, it pulled Grandfather apart. His insides dropped to the stones beneath them. His screams died. Silence fell on the mountain, save for the crunches of Grandfather's bones as the giant devoured him with its massive maw.

Warm air from behind me pulled my hair back and forth. I stood rooted to the spot. One of those creatures was behind me. It took a great inhale, ingesting my scent. My whole body trembled. I shut my eyes, waiting for my turn to be swallowed.

"Your smell is like us," a deep voice rumbled behind me.

I blinked a few times, heart lodged in my throat. I slowly turned around and came face to face with a giant woman.

Her features were rough around the edges, as if carved in stone, the eyes beady and black as beetles. Her teeth as sharp as mine. I looked down and let out a soft gasp. Hooves for legs.

"You're like me?"

The woman nodded, and her face split into a yellowed, toothy grin.

The ground quaked as the male giant—or was it a troll?—lumbered towards us. He smacked his lips and licked his bloody fingers.

"So, you're not going to eat me, like you did with my grandfather?" I glanced around the area, to see if there were any remains of him. Nothing but blood spatters painting red dots to the white canvas.

The troll woman shook her head. "We don't kill our own."

Heat rose behind my eyelids. Our own? Was I really a creature like them? I wished my mother was still alive. She would have told me the truth. Yet, I felt a floating sensation within me, as if all of the world's burden had been lifted off my shoulders. I licked my lips with cautious hope. At that same moment, my stomach rumbled. I wrapped my arms around my midsection, blushing.

The troll couple chuckled. The woman bent down to a small, woolen bag beside an actual boulder, opened it and handed me a sweet-smelling object.

My mouth filled with saliva at the heady scent, yet I hesitated. "What is it?"

"Food," she said simply.

It looked like dried meat. I hadn't had meat in such a long time. My grandparents always fed me scraps or what they couldn't finish. I chewed a bite off it, savoring the salty yet sweet flavor in my mouth. It tasted nothing like the stringy, musty flavor of grass that came from mutton. "What kind of meat is it?"

"Human," the troll man said with a grin.

I stiffened and stared at the strip of meat in my hand. I wanted to be revolted. I expected to puke it all out. My stomach fluttered for a brief moment before it gave away to pure, primal hunger. Drool dripping from my teeth, I shoved the rest of the strips into my mouth and chewed. I'd never imagined humans tasted so good. The troll man patted my head with his massive palm when I licked my fingers clean. Looking up, there was a genuine smile on his face. I'd never seen such mirth being directed at me before.

The troll woman fastened the bag on her shoulder and knelt in front of me, her arms flung to either side. "Come."

"Where?" I asked.

"Home."

Her chest was warm as she embraced me. I had never been held like that. I swallowed the lump in my throat. Home sounded good. "Will you give me more of that meat if I come with you?"

The troll man barked with laughter. "As much as you want. Now's the time they wander up the mountain in search of their sheep. We'll get plenty."

I nodded, nuzzling in the crook of the troll woman's neck. Every bit of misery accumulated throughout the years of abuse and neglect seemed to evaporate out of my system. For the first time in my life, I felt safe. Accepted. Excited for the future.

"What is your name, child?"

My grandparents had never given me one. Didn't even christen me out of fear I'd burn the church down. They, along with the others in the village, called me all sorts of names, but one always stuck. It seemed to bring loathing and terror as soon as they had the courage to utter it. Perhaps that would stay like that as I grew up, with their own flesh sustaining me. Making me bigger and stronger. Making me the terrifying legend that I am today.

"Grýla."

SURVIVAL OF THE FITTEST

Val clambered out of the cave that had been her home for the past few months, carrying a worn leather knapsack. The acrid air that hung stagnant burned holes in her lungs. Her bare skin prickled, as if the radiation was seeping into her like fine mist. She quickly grabbed a couple of wet wipes from her bag and scrubbed the nuclear particles from her face and arms. Without a proper shower, it was the only thing she could do to fend off the fallout.

At least Val seemed more fortunate than the rest of the world. Everything around her lay scorched after the blast.

Thick, gray clouds blocked all sunlight and the temperature had dropped about twenty digits since she went into hibernation. The increasing cold and lack of sunshine didn't bother Val when she'd been alive and certainly didn't bother her now when she traipsed the thin line between life and death.

Val looked at what remained that had concealed her safe haven. Four months ago, the forest had been lush with ash trees, cottonwood and pecan trees. Val had enjoyed taking walks through the area, ingraining in her memory the places where poison ivy hid between the trees like a patient predator, how the leaves changed from green to a pinkish hue and then settling on indigo during twilight hours and of course, appreciating the ample amount of nourishment in the form of wildlife the forest provided. The white-tailed deer had been a delicacy that Val had particularly enjoyed when she couldn't bother to go to the nearest town.

Now, however, the forest was speckled with gaping wounds from where the trees had been ripped off its roots. Charcoal and contaminated dirt littered the ground. Not a footprint in sight.

Val heaved a big sigh that transformed into a dry cough, like she had inhaled a bucket of sand. She ran her tingling tongue over her aching teeth and blinked away the dark spots that popped in the peripheral of her vision. Her supplies had run out a few days ago, but she had remained inside the cavern out of sheer stubbornness, thinking she could overpower her need for sustenance.

Now she was reaping what she had sowed.

Charred branches and dried animal carcasses crunched beneath Val's feet. No matter where she looked, death looked back with a bleak silence.

That was what bothered her the most. Even at night, when she did most of the hunting, the forest had been teeming with life; crickets buzzed on the bark and her fellow nocturnal creatures, like bobcats and coyotes, prowled between the trees. Listening to the endearing sounds of a family of bobcats had been an entertaining delight to Val when the hand crank radio wasn't working. Even the hiss of a wind when it breezed past her let her know if people were camping in the woods.

A sliver of dread crept down Val's back. Would she be able to find food here? Perhaps not. She doubted people had thought of seeking refuge in the numerous caverns in Tennessee before the blast. Too far away from civilization.

Val gritted her teeth. As much as she hated it, she had no choice but to leave her beloved mountain and venture to the nearest town. All for the sake of surviving. That's what she has done for the past fifty years, after she shed her mortal coil and accepted life after death.

"You'll find food soon," she said out loud, not to comfort herself, but to destroy the silence that threatened to choke her. "And once you've found food, then you can plan the next step."

Feeling more spirited, Val tread down the beaten path and tried to ignore the constricting feeling in her chest as the forest thinned and gave way to asphalt roads, deserted burnt cars, and desolation. She hummed "Let it Be", a song that reminded her of days past, of opulence, apathy, and greed. The walk down memory lane turned dark as she remembered the heated tension between the two biggest nations in the world. How the empty threats filled powder kegs of danger until they inevitably exploded. There was no "if", only "when" the end of civilization began. Days before the eventual blast, like a dog that sensed earthquake before it hit, Val had prepared herself, raided the nearest blood bank, taken all the blood from the refrigerators, and headed off to the mountains. She had found the situation kind of funny as she got comfortable in the darkest regions of the cavern. Her friend Sam would have laughed at her survival tactics. Val paused, a pang of worry hitting her core. Had her friend sought shelter in time? Val banished the thoughts. They had gone their separate ways years ago, due to Sam discovering Val's true nature, and Val had been fine with it. Creatures like her were better off alone. Besides, there would always be plenty of people to mingle with later on.

Val scoffed now while kicking a scorched human skull that bounced on the asphalt, eventually stopping at a mangled car. Everywhere she looked, devastation reared its ugly head.

The town was in no better shape than the forest. Crumbling buildings and bright embers from burning tires flanked Val on both sides. The radiation was so cloying she thought she saw actual vibrations in the air. She scratched at a dry spot on her knuckle and stopped abruptly, staring at her hand. Would her skin break out into oozing lesions if she stepped further into town?

Was it worth it?

Cursing under her breath, she ripped a piece of her sweater and wrapped it around her face. Not that it would do much in the end, but it would have to suffice while she searched for food. She had to stay hopeful, or else the crippling loneliness would squeeze out the last dredges of her sanity.

Spotting the piles of skeletal bodies strewn around the streets like garbage, Val felt her hope dwindle. Where would she find food in this wasteland?

Val's throat began to itch from dryness. It was as if spikes were growing from the soft tissue within, burrowing out. Fearing they were growing and would block her airways, she bit into the palm of her hand and suckled on what little dripped from the wound. Her own cold, thick blood was nothing compared to the warmth of a living being, or even a day-old body that still kept the blood's nutrients fresh for scavengers. None of that was here, however, so her own blood kept the hunger preoccupied until she found a hospital or a clinic. They always kept some in store in case of emergencies.

"Well, this is a goddamn emergency," Val rasped, and marched on.

She found a small clinic after a half-hour trek through the town. The windows were smashed and the building reeked of death. Chances were low that she'd find anyone alive inside, but as long as their blood hadn't become congealed sludge, she could feed.

Val sidestepped overturned gurneys, the mattresses black from extinguished flames, and broken heart monitors. Somebody had already raided the pharmacy corner, cabinets mocking her with their empty maws. Val didn't care about drugs, but it did give her hope that there was life in this town after all. The cooler at the back of the clinic where they kept the refrigerated medicine had long been shut down. No cool air embraced Val when she opened the door. Only the dank, curdled odor of expired drugs assaulted her senses. She wrinkled her nose under the face cloth and ignored the damp packages on the shelves. To the left, two stainless steel refrigerators lined the wall at the end of the room. Remembering the ones she'd raided before the blast, Val knew what she would find inside: A whole buffet of O, A, B, and AB blood. Elation and relief drove her forward and she almost tore the door off in her excitement. A rancid, metallic stench kicked Val backwards. The blood bags lying on the plastic shelves were brown in color. Spoilt beyond salvation.

Val's scoff turned into mirthless chuckle. The power was off. Of course it would go bad. She threw the useless sustenance onto the floor and stomped on the bags till the brown sludge burst out and spattered everything in dead gore.

Val threw her head back and screamed. A raw, primal, hungry one.

It's not fair, she thought and fought the angry tears that threatened to spill. She stumbled out of the cooler, feeling more vulnerable than a deer facing a raging car. Darkness had begun smudging the edges of her vision. Her teeth ached more than ever. Dizziness and black-out would soon take over and blur what logic conveyed in her mind. She'd end up roaming the country a feral beast until she starved to death or ended up eating herself.

She wondered if it would be better to lock herself in the cooler when she heard it.

A scream.

A *human* scream.

It came from a few blocks away. A cry for help, it seemed.

Val didn't care. Food was food. She sprinted in the direction her meal was hiding.

The origin of the scream rebounded from a cluttered alley between what used to be a flower shop and an antique store. Nothing but scorched trash remained.

Nothing alive.

There was someone clinging to life in the alley, though. Desperately fighting for it, judging from the hoarse screams.

Val's mouth filled with saliva as she pictured herself plunging her teeth into that neck, consuming the crimson that pumped life into those meatbags. She would have her fill and then collect the remaining blood into jars for later.

She screeched to a halt, shoes sliding slightly on the wet asphalt.

A young girl in a wheelchair lay sideways on the ground while fending off an attack from a very malnourished coyote. The animal was just skin and bones, on the same hunt for food as Val. It had its teeth on the girl's ankle and tried with all its measly might to drag her out of the wheelchair. Val used its preoccupation to her advantage. She pounced on the coyote, teeth bared, and threw it against the brick wall. It gave a pained yelp, but before it got up, Val had her hands on its neck. She snapped it without hesitation and buried her face into its furry back before the body got cold. The warmth from the blood gave her goosebumps and she sucked it dry. Its blood, however, contained traces of radiation. It soured the nutrients and altered the once sweet iron taste into bitter almond flavor, reminiscent of cyanide. Val almost gagged while slurping the last drops, but she forced it down.

It would have to do until she fed from the human.

Feeling somewhat let down, but a bit sated, she dropped the carcass on the ground, wiped the blood and matted fur from her face and turned to the girl. Got a *good* look at her next meal.

The coyote's blood churned in Val's stomach.

It hadn't been the coyote that had beaten Val to the punch. It was the goddamn radiation.

Red welts covered almost every inch of the girl's skin, like someone had splashed acid on her. She was almost bald, with clumps of hair clinging to her scarred scalp. Her bottom lip looked as if it had already burst; crusts of caked blood dotted around her mouth. Despite the horrendous features, a hopeful glint gleamed in her inflamed eyes.

What a pitiful creature.

Val gritted her teeth, swallowing the curse that danced on her tongue. Just her fucking luck.

"Thank you," the girl rasped in short, rattling breaths while struggling to adjust the chair. The effort brought forth a coughing fit that seemed to last a lifetime.

Val instinctively stepped back, as if afraid the girl's toxic phlegm would spatter on her. It was bad enough the coyote's toxic blood was circulating in her system at the moment. Then she felt a twinge of guilt. Cursing under her breath, Val crouched beside the girl and helped her to a sitting position, though she was careful to touch the tatters of fabric that clung to the girl's skeletal frame. The girl trembled viciously, out of fear, cold or radiation poisoning, Val didn't know. Maybe it was all of the above.

"There, is that better?" Val asked as she rubbed her hands liberally on her jeans, already feeling the pin and needles piercing her fingertips. She should get the hell out of there, before she too succumbed to the horrible toxicity that was killing her meal.

"Are you going to eat me too?" the girl asked quietly once her breathing got stable.

Val blinked. It wasn't the question that struck her. The tone of the girl's voice hinted at hope, almost yearning. Hadn't she screamed herself raw for help as the coyote clamped its mouth on her ankle? Murky blood trickled from the wound, oozing like strawberry jelly. The smell of iron was usually too tantalizing for Val to handle, but it smelled corrupted now. Like spiked Kool-Aid. She knew she'd choke on the blood if she consumed it.

Val shook her head. "I want to, believe me. I've come a long way to search for food, but I can't. The radiation has damaged the quality." She winced at the poor choice of words. It *has* been a long time since her last communication with another living being.

The girl gave a slow nod, as if accepting her slow, torturous death sentence. The light in her eyes was fading. Val concentrated her hearing on the girl's heartbeat. It was slow. There wasn't much time. Did the girl know? Was that why she had asked Val that question?

"Why are you out here, anyway?" Val asked. "This isn't exactly the ideal environment for … uh." She gestured at the wheelchair.

The girl scoffed and her bony fists clutched the armrests. "I was in a bunker not far from here. The residents thought I was a useless burden on their little underground society and they cast me out."

That whole sentence seemed too much for her fragile lungs and she launched into another coughing fit. Bloody phlegm smeared her palm when it subsided.

Guilt wrapped around Val's guts like thorny vines. Even though she would never admit this to the girl, Val had been one of the despicable nocturnes that had preyed on disabled people. They were easy to kill, simple as that. She never stopped and asked them their name before taking their lives. If that girl's blood hadn't been contaminated, Val probably wouldn't have hesitated to kill her. Should she show mercy and finish the job? It would be easy, just a quick snap of the neck, like the coyote.

Val shook her head, banishing the temptation from her mind. No. That girl had already been abandoned by her own kin. She had no one. Just like Val.

Val straightened and began walking away.

The girl looked up and let out a mirthless chuckle. "Thanks for saving me, I guess."

Seeing the item she was looking for, Val bent down and picked up a busted, aluminum trash can. She carried it to where the girl was sitting and placed it beside the wheelchair. Then she took a seat.

The girl raised an eyebrow—Val noticed how the burnt skin arched upward. "What are you doing?"

Val sighed. "Look, I'm not a good person. I've ended a lot of lives, all in the good ol' name of survival, and it didn't faze me. It's just how it works, you know? Survival of the fittest and all that crap."

The girl frowned. "If you're trying to cheer me up or something, you're failing—hard."

Val ruffled her hair in frustration, teeth grinding. She *really* wasn't good at this. "What I'm trying to say, is that I don't usually help people unless I get something out of it. Like now, I thought I'd get to end my hunger with your blood. Obviously, that's not going to happen, so I should walk away, right? Find another source of nourishment."

The girl cocked her head to the side. "Then why don't you?"

Val blew raspberries and with a shrug, looked at the girl. *Really* looked at her. No aversion of the eyes or pretending the girl doesn't exist. "Because I can't let you die out here all alone. No one deserves that."

The girl stared at Val in disbelief. "Then are you going to be with me until I croak? Might be a long time till then." Her chuckle mutated into a grotesque rattle. Her chest heaved with each breath, like she was trying to push a boulder off of it.

Val knew that she knew she didn't have long. Maybe just a day. Val nodded. "I've got all the time in the world. Do you have a favorite place around here?"

The girl thought for a moment. "Yeah."

Val rose and took the wheelchair handles into her hands. "Then, show me."

Val didn't expect the girl to take her to the local cemetery. She'd thought her home would be a better place, or hell, even a nice public park.

"Why here?" she asked as she parked the chair up against the remains of a great willow tree, its empty branches crackling by the simplest touch.

The girl shrugged. "It's peaceful here."

Val had to admit she was right. Unlike the rest of the town, it wasn't surrounded with destroyed vehicles and debris. Although morbid and enveloped in death, the tombstones that cluttered the area gave off a sense of tranquility that Val had never noticed before. To many, a place like this was their final resting place on Earth. Yet even in death, the deceased had loved ones who had mourned their departure and found time to visit the graves and keep them beautiful.

Val glanced down at the girl. Was that the reason she wanted to be here? For this place to be *her* final resting place? Did she have someone who would mourn her? Was her family even alive? Val refrained from asking her those questions. Why twist the knife when the wound was still bleeding?

"What's your name?" Val asked.

"Phoebe."

Val smiled. "I'm Val. Despite the circumstances, it's nice to meet you, Phoebe."

The girl nodded. Her eyelids fluttered, as if they weighted a ton. Staying awake was getting too tiresome for her frail body.

Knowing her name wasn't enough for Val, though. She had to know everything about Phoebe, before it was too late.

"Hey, what's your favorite TV show?" Val asked.

Phoebe raised an eyebrow. "Why do you wanna know?"

Val shrugged. "Humor me."

Phoebe was quick with an answer. "Glee."

Val had no idea what kind of show that was, so she couldn't expand on her question. "What about your favorite book?"

"*Hitchhiker's Guide to the Galaxy,*" Phoebe replied, smirking.

Val perked up. "Hey, I know that one! I listened to the 1978 radio broadcast while I was hitchhiking across Britain!"

Phoebe's eyes widened in wonderment. "Really? I've read all the books and seen the movie. The books are so much better, right?"

Val nodded, elation coursing through her veins. "Nothing beats the books."

A connection was forming between them, Val felt it. She hadn't realized how much she had missed it. "What about music?"

Phoebe opened her mouth to answer, but she erupted in rattling coughs. Her shoulders quaked with the effort of holding still in her chair. Without hesitation, Val reached down and wiped the bloodied phlegm from Phoebe's mouth when she became too tired. Val's skin didn't explode into goosebumps at the touch. She chided herself for the fearful callousness earlier.

"Why are you asking me all this?" Phoebe asked, panting.

"Isn't it obvious?"

Phoebe shook her head.

Val sighed. "Because I want to honor the memory of the only friend I've had in a long time. I want something to remember you by as I roam around this fucking wasteland."

Phoebe scoffed. "Selfish," she muttered, but a small smile tugged at her swollen lips.

"We are selfish creatures, after all."

Since talking was taking a toll on Phoebe, it was Val's turn. She shared her life experiences with the girl, though she bypassed much of the bloodshed as possible. She regaled Phoebe with stories of the hippie movement of the sixties and seventies; how much the free-spirited folks had been generous with their blood without them really knowing.

"What does that mean?" Phoebe asked.

Val grinned, showing her teeth. "Well, let's just say a lot of them were too high on drugs to notice my neck kisses bit too deep."

"Oh." Phoebe made a face and Val quickly changed the subject to stories about how she had hitchhiked across the country at least four times and had reveled in the wisdom people taught her.

"Did you see any of those people again?" Phoebe asked.

Val gazed into the horizon. She could almost smell the menthol tobacco from Sam as her mind traveled to the past. "Yeah. I met a woman named Sam during my first trip and we made it a tradition to travel together when we could. Those were good times."

She looked at Phoebe and smiled. It felt good to have someone to listen. Sometimes that was enough. "But I'm also having a good time now."

Phoebe was about to return the smile when one of her coughing fits burst out. The most violent one that Val had seen. Phoebe's entire body convulsed and jerked in the chair, her limbs flailing as if electrocuted. Blackened blood spewed in abstract spatters on the ground.

Stomach plummeting, Val grabbed hold of Phoebe's arms and held the girl tight. The pulse got weaker and weaker. The skin grew colder.

"No, no, no, no," Val whispered, eyes wide. "You can't go now. Hold on a little longer, please?"

Phoebe offered her a weak smile, teeth stained in blood and black mucus. She craned her neck and whispered something in Val's ear.

Val's brow furrowed. Why was she telling her that?

Phoebe squeezed Val's hand one last time and uttered the same words she said to her when they met. "Thank you."

Blisters pulsed on Val's palms, on the verge of popping, but Val didn't care.

She didn't care that radioactive dirt smeared her clothes. Her cheeks were wet with tears, but she didn't wipe them away. She stomped on the cemetery ground, making sure it was even and then fetched the makeshift cross she'd made out of the wooden tool shed. What was left of it, anyways.

She drove it deep into the grave, not stopping until it stood level and straight. It took a few attempts, but it wasn't like she was in any hurry. Then using one of her claws, she sliced into her right index finger and wrote Phoebe's name on the cross.

"Here lies Phoebe. A good person and a friend."

Val considered saying something after the burial, but it wasn't necessary. There was no one here who would listen.

But she knew where she could find some. Phoebe had told her. In her time of death, she'd made sure that Val would survive.

Val sniffed and hoisted the beat-up wheelchair up on her shoulder.

"Well, time to eat."

They Came from the Rocks

[The following e-mail exchange comes from contractor Gestur Hilmarsson and Álfaljós's liaison Hörður Bjarnason before the events of March 21st and Gestur's subsequent disappearance.]

Date: 02/27/2026
Time: 17:15 p.m.
From: Gestur Hilmarsson <gesturgverktakar.is>
To: Hörður Bjarnason <hordur@alfaljos.is>
Subject: First drill operation

Good afternoon, Hörður,

I hope you are well.

In accordance with our contract, I am to give you small briefs into the project.

I'm pleased to announce my team managed to put the first drill through the rocks below the glacier. The fumes from the magma have even gone to the top, so it's safe to say we've reached our destination.

It wasn't easy, though. Those rocks are ancient, might be even older than our settlement according to the geologist, and they're sturdier than steel. Hell, it took us quite a while to crack through the ice. Most of our machines came close to malfunctioning the deeper and closer we got to the crust. Unfortunately, two of the three titanium-coated drills that we received from your company dismantled from our machine. We have no idea how it happened, but it seems to have occurred around the same time the first drill broke through the rocks (see attached the video footage from the surveillance camera). Geiri, my engineer, and Konráð, my mechanic, tried to fix it but to no avail. I think you mentioned during the orientation that you have specialists that could help? If so, that'd be great.

Other than that slight malfunction, everything is going according to plan.

Between you and me, though? This project is one of the weirdest ones I've done. Not that I disagree with its objective. After the sudden increase in population, we're in dire need of other methods of extracting electricity from what nature can provide for us. Hydroelectric just doesn´t cut it anymore. It's why I was intrigued by Álfaljós and their innovative approach to renew geothermal energy. I hope you've been ignoring those protesters parked in front of the company. I know I would, and I'm relieved they're not stupid enough to protest in the middle of the glacier. They're just afraid of change, that's all. And it's a necessary change, mind you.

Speaking of change, some of my more old-fashioned men have been somewhat reluctant to disturb the natural geography, saying we're being hypocrites if we're fining foreign tourists for off-road driving that destroys our moss but we're getting scot-free from drilling into our own glaciers. I pressed them about the actual issue and they mumbled something about the ones who were before us would not like what we're doing. Just plain, old superstition, I suppose. I reminded them of their wages and the benefits Álfaljós provided them and that seemed to have shut them up. I'm sure it's nothing to worry about, but I still wanted to let you know.

I also want to let you know that not a day goes by that I'm grateful Álfaljós liked the quota from my company. That I'm part of changing the lives of Icelanders for the better makes my heart swell with pride.

I apologize if it sounds like I've been babbling. I have no idea what to put in these briefs.

Anyway, if you could send over your specialist in the next couple of days, we can resume the drilling and advance to the next stage.

Looking forward to hearing from you.

Regards,
Gestur.

Date: 02/28/2026
Time: 14:12 p.m.
From: Hörður Bjarnason <hordur@alfaljos.is>
To: Gestur Hilmarsson <gestur@gverktakar.is>
Subject: Congrats on the first drill!

Good afternoon, Gestur,

I'm delighted to hear that your team has penetrated the first barrier of our initiative. It won't take too long for the second act to begin, I presume. I'm unsure if I have contacted the manufacturer in China already about the titanium pipes shipment, but I estimate it will arrive in Iceland in four to six weeks, judging how the weather will fare overseas. I can't wait to relay the first success to our CEO. I'm sure she will be thrilled.

You need not worry about those protesters. Sure, they are pesky and are worried that we are hurting the environment. One such "carer for the environment" even emailed me, saying that nature would pay us back threefold if we were to mess with it. Can you believe that? But it's all right. I pity them, actually. They only worry about the present. They don't care about the future like we at Álfaljós do. Or at least they don't care enough to plan a proper living for their children and their children's children. Because that's what we are doing. Making sure that Iceland will be habitable in places like the highlands without the worry of the forces of nature. I'm glad you see it that way as well, Gestur.

I appreciate you notifying me about the superstitions from your men, by the way. The old ways can be hard to let go and the same goes for superstitions, I'm afraid. Hell, I'm not afraid to admit that I never walk under a ladder or I usually knock on wood to ward off any jinxes. It's part of being a silly human. But as long as your men do their work diligently, then we need not to worry.

So, you need a specialist? Say no more. I know just the man appropriate for the job. His name is Atli Erlendsson and he's one of the engineers who developed the drills for the project. I'll request a transfer for him later today. I expect he'll reach your destination within the next twenty-four hours or so. He's one of the best, I'm sure you're going to like him.

I do appreciate these briefs from you, Gestur, and I look forward to receiving more of them in the coming weeks.

Have a nice day.

All the best,
Hörður.

Date: 03/03/2026
Time: 18:05 p.m.
From: Gestur Hilmarsson <gestur@gverktakar.is>
To: Hörður Bjarnason <hordur@alfaljos.is>
Subject: Many thanks

Good afternoon, Hörður.

I want to thank you for sending over Atli, the specialist, so quickly. The storm last week delayed his arrival, but once the fog cleared up, everything was fine. He immediately detected the problem of the drills' dismantling and set out to work, borrowing both my engineer and mechanic for assistance. I was amazed by his efficiency.

You're not going to keep him forever, right? Because there just might be a position available for him on my team. Atli informed me the repairs would take a day or two, and I told him to take as much time as he'd need since we've been ahead of schedule for a couple of weeks thanks to the lull in weather on the glacier.

He's a good kid and I'm once again grateful for having him here. In fact, he's fitting in nicely with the others. He informed me the evening he arrived that some of the men told him to keep himself on his toes when he goes down below. When he asked them why, they simply said they felt like they were being watched. I laughed at this and pointed to all the cameras that are in every nook and cranny in the facility as well as down where the drill is. I'm sure they meant that I will be watching him through the surveillance.

Anyway, I will send you a report of the repairs once he's finished.

Take care.
Gestur.

Date: 03/04/2026
Time: 08:37 a.m.
From: Hörður Bjarnason <hordur@alfaljos.is>
To: Gestur Hilmarsson <gestur@gverktakar.is>
Subject: Not for sale ;)

Greetings, Gestur,

I told you he's one of the best. And I'm afraid we intend to keep him in our company for a very long time. You can't have him just yet.

But who knows, if he enjoys being on your team, he's free to go over to your side. No hard feelings on our end if that happens.

I look forward to reading your repairs report once I've had my technical specialist deciphered for me. I hope you won't spread it around that I´m not as tech savvy as the rest of you, haha.

Have a nice day.

Regards,
Hörður.

Date: 03/04/2026
Time: 18:05 p.m.
From: Gestur Hilmarsson <gestur@gverktakar.is>
To: Hörður Bjarnason <hordur@alfaljos.is>
Subject: Unfortunate accident

Dear Hörður,

I'm sorry to say this, but Atli has been in a terrible accident. You've probably gotten wind of it already since the medic in the helicopter transporting him to Reykjavík hospital requested all his contact information.

Still, I want to give you my report of what happened. Then hopefully Atli can fill in the blanks once he wakes up from his drug-induced coma …

We were in shortwave radio contact the entire time as the drills are located deep under the glacier. Surveillance cameras are there, as you remember from the footage I sent you last week, but the connection has been crap as of late. No idea why, but the resolution has been very grainy most of the time. What's important is, I had eyes and ears on him throughout his initial inspection and subsequent repair.

It was around three in the afternoon yesterday when he told my engineer and mechanic to go fetch additional equipment and extra pipes from the small warehouse we keep in the main building above ground. I asked Atli if he was all right working by himself. He just smiled with a silly wave into the camera before turning his back to me and resuming his work.

I can't remember if you went on the tour the day the project began, but the steel lanes are all fastened into the ice itself with a mixture of rods and marine epoxy. It's a weird combo, I know, but it works and hasn't failed us yet.

Until yesterday, that is.

I can´t quite explain it—my eyes must have been playing tricks on me, or I was just too exhausted, but it *seemed* like something crawled *underneath* the lane Atli stood on. It wasn't some animal as there are no animals up on the goddamn glacier.

I radioed Atli to see if he saw anything. He humored me by looking around but found nothing in the end. It must have been a trick of the atrociously bad lighting down there. I watched Atli work on the drills for about an hour when something completely obscured the camera lens. It wasn't the occasional sleet that slurries down into the cracks. It seemed more solid—I thought for a second it was the palm of someone's hand, which is silly of course.

Then the screams crackled through the shortwave radio.

My heart shot up in panic waves. The cameras either showed static or darkness. I called for Atli, asking if everything was all right. I received nothing but agonizing screams in return.

I contacted Geiri and told him and Konráð to go check on Atli. Something was very much wrong here.

I waited in an anxiety-induced puddle of sweat, staring at the monitor screen, wishing it'd go back online.

As if on cue, the surveillance feed fell back into place.

I wish now it hadn't. I would have been spared the image forever burned in my brain.

The spare rods and pipes Atli had brought with him pierced his entire body. Some of them bent through the steel grid at different angles, fastening the poor man deeper into the lane. Despite the bad resolution I detected no blood pouring from the multiple wounds. It's as if he had been *merged* with the lane, turning him into this grotesque abstract art display from hell.

It took all my men six hours to cut the rods out of his body. He was conscious the entire time. His screams reached the main building above ground.

I'm so sorry. This is all my fault. If I had been there to supervise in person, this probably wouldn't have happened. I take full responsibility for my carelessness and Álfaljós may direct Atli's hospital bills to me.

God, I hope he pulls through the operation.

No one deserves this much pain.

I'll give a more detailed report when I head back to Reykjavík in the coming weeks after I have reexamined the surveillance tapes and conducted a safety procedure on the steel lanes. Please keep me informed on Atli's well-being in the meantime.

Regards,
Gestur.

Date: 03/08/2026
Time: 16:29 p.m.
From: Hörður Bjarnason <hordur@alfaljos.is>
To: Gestur Hilmarsson <gestur@gverktakar.is>
Subject: Concerning Atli's well-being

Greetings, Gestur,

I want to inform you that Atli's operation went well. It took over 12 hours, but the doctors managed to pull out the shrapnel from the pipes out of his body without causing too much damage to the muscle tissues. He's going to need extensive physical and mental therapy but he's a trooper. I'm certain he will pull through.

The CEO and I went to visit him two days after the operation. He seemed weak, covered from head to toe in bandages and tubes pumping fluids into his body. But he responded well to our gifts, he even managed a raspy chuckle at the gray colored éclair his department sent him.

I'm worried about his mental health, though. After the CEO left, I probed him for answers on the day of the accident. I wanted to know what had really happened below the glacier, since you haven't sent me the report yet (there's no need to rush, of course). However, as soon as I mentioned the steel lane, Atli's eyes bulged out of his sockets, and he gurgled a terrified shriek. His whole body shook violently. I was afraid the tethers that held his legs and arms up would snap. He mouthed something I couldn't hear or understand. The nurses ushered me out of his room before I could lean down and listen to what he had to say.

The doctor explained to me Atli was still in shock after the accident and that his brain was still processing the event and its aftermath. I would have to allow him more rest before I could ask him further questions.

It's frustrating, especially if there's any reason to believe that you and your crew are working in an unsafe environment. Which shouldn't be, given the report you sent me at the start of this year.

I'd appreciate it if you could continue to send me reports—any kind, environmental, weather, morale, whatever you can think of—over the next days.

It would certainly put my mind at ease as well as the CEO's.

Take care of yourself.

All the best,

Hörður.

Date: 03/10/2026
Time: 17:38 p.m.
Frm: Gestur Hilmarsson <gestur@gverktakar.is>
To: Hörður Bjarnason <hordur@alfaljos.is>
Subject: Reporting another "incident"

Afternoon, Hörður,

Thank you for keeping me posted about Atli. I'm relieved to hear the operation went well. I really hope he recovers fast from that horrific ordeal. I wish my e-mails would bring you some good news as well, but sadly no.

My team has been acting … odd, as of late. They've become more tired and quick to anger. When I ask them what the problem is, they all tell me they can't sleep because of the voices. I bet you're confused because I sure am. I asked them what kind of voices are keeping them up all night, but they can't explain it to me. Sometimes it's whispers that slither down their ears or other nights they're covering their heads with pillows because they claim something is shrieking in the walls. My quarters aren't in the same building, unfortunately, so I haven't heard anything at all. I've examined the cameras that are installed in the sleeping quarters and they haven't picked up any sound, except for the men's snores.

I've tried to shorten their shifts so they can go to bed earlier, but it doesn't seem to work. They all sport dark circles under their eyes and grouchy attitudes each morning. Most of them wish to go home during the weekends, but I've told them it's not part of their contract. It's not going to look good for us if we delay the project any further than it already has, what with Atli's unfortunate accident.

In order to come to some sort of a compromise, I promised them I would check with you if it was possible to slightly raise their wages, or at the very least, allow them a weekend off once a month.

Let me know what you think.

Regards,
Gestur

Date: 03/11/2026
Time: 16:29 p.m.
From: Hörður Bjarnason <hordur@alfaljos.is>
To: Gestur Hilmarsson <gestur@gverktakar.is>
Subject: A Good Compromise!

Greetings, Gestur,

It's awful to hear that your men aren't getting enough rest. A good night's sleep does wonder to you, especially when you're working hard in a difficult terrain. The weather on the glacier has hardly been getting any better, so I'm certain they've just been hearing the howling of the wind each night.

I brought up your idea to the CEO in our weekly meetings and she wasn't against the pay raise idea at all. I'll need to confirm with the financial department, but I'm assuming we might be able to raise the wages to about 5-10%, depending on expertise and so on.

As for the weekend trips, we'll have to wait a bit before we can decide on that. The CEO wants to see how far we progress with the project for another month or two. If everything is going well and ahead of schedule, we can definitely plan a weekend getaway for your team.

But for now, I hope your men will be pleased to get more money for their work. For sake of Iceland's future, they certainly deserve it.

Please, continue to send me reports and I will do my best to navigate through any concerns you or your crew might have.

All the best,
Hörður

Date: 03/13/2026
Time: 17:38 p.m.
From: Gestur Hilmarsson <gestur@gverktakar.is>
To: Hörður Bjarnason <hordur@alfaljos.is>
Subject: My team is getting on my nerves

Afternoon, Hörður,

I don't know what to tell you. The subject of today's report is what it is. They're getting on my nerves with their constant whining. A couple of days ago, I told you of their bad sleep schedule and how much that has affected their work.

Well, now they've been coming to me almost hourly with various complaints: The lift isn't working, their equipment has gone missing or they find it at the most ridiculous places. Magni, our welder, for example, lost his welding equipment and spent the entire day searching for it, only for him to find it in the kitchen! The guys must have been playing a prank on him, but they swore they didn't touch it. I don't know who to believe because cameras didn't catch anything.

Sævar and Leifur, two of my older associates, are getting spooked. They spotted some weird-looking footprints in the snow, in front of the glacier opening. They keep muttering about the ones who lived before us and that we should leave this instant. When the rest of us went outside to check them out, there was nothing there. When I asked them who "they" are, they just shook their heads, as if they were disappointed that I don't know what they're talking about. What's worse, my threats about cutting their pay isn't reaching to them anymore. The others have caught them talking about leaving the facility once the weather clears, and I'm not even sure if I want to stop them.

I can't have superstitious quitters on my team.

This might just be a bad week. Everyone has those from time to time. Hopefully, things will get better soon.

Sorry for the nagging report.

Regards,
Gestur

Date: 03/14/2026
Time: 17:38 p.m.
From: Gestur Hilmarsson <gestur@gverktakar.is>
To: Hörður Bjarnason <hordur@alfaljos.is>
Subject: Requesting new crew

Afternoon, Hörður,

There's no easy way to say this: I've lost some of my men.

I have no idea where they've gone. What I *do* know is they must have left in a hurry because all their belongings are still in their cabins above ground. I suspect they must have been spooked by Konráð's ridiculous story. It's probably nothing, but he claims to have seen some kind of *creatures* climb through the miniscule cracks in both the glacier and the rock behind it. It was only for a second and when he went to check again, they were gone, as if melted into the ice. Like I said, it's ridiculous. I've told Konráð that Álfaljós won't tolerate these kinds of tall tales and that I would dock some of the hours from his wages if he continued to spread them. That seemed to have shut him up.

But it still doesn't explain the absence of my trusty men. Like Sævar and Leifur, for example. They're like me; old-fashioned, efficient and we take no bullshit at our jobs. I know I reported in the previous email that they'd been talking of leaving, but they wouldn't leave their stuff behind.

I don't know what can explain this. We *have* been away from home for two months now, however. Homesickness must have caught up to them. It happens to all of us. I freely admit I miss my children and I've got no one at home to warm my sheets, but I've got a project to supervise, and I won't be able to keep up with the schedule if none of my men will work. The ones who haven't deserted me, Geir and Konráð included, took the snowmobiles and cruised around the facility and its surroundings to see if they stumbled upon a lone straggler, shivering in their boots, but so far, no such luck. I investigated the surveillance footage, but no dice. We bought those cameras a month ago and they're supposed to be state of the art, but the resolution is absolute shit. It's like there's a blizzard within the facilities (see attached clips).

I hate asking this of you, but I'd appreciate it if you could send over a new crew, one that preferably doesn't believe in superstitious crap. It wouldn't hurt to ship over new surveillance cameras as well.

I'm sure Álfaljós wants us to finish the project as soon as possible but I can't do that unless I get more people over here.

Hope to hear from you soon.

Regards,
Gestur.

[Video Attachment, titled „Surveillance – crew dorms 03/08/2026" 10MB]
[Video Attachment, titled „Surveillance – crew dorms 03/09/2026" 10MB]

Date: 03/15/2026
Time: 11:45 a.m.
From: Hörður Bjarnason <hordur@alfaljos.is>
To: Gestur Hilmarsson <gestur@gverktakar.is>
Subject: Regarding "missing crew"

Greetings, Gestur,

Is everything okay over there?

I tried calling you as soon as I got your email yesterday, but you didn't answer your phone. I understand you've been quite busy since some of your crew seems to have left the facilities.

I looked at the video clips you sent me. You're right, the resolution was really bad, but with the help from the guys at IT, they managed to clear the resolution to a point where I could see obvious shapes of the human kind, if you catch my drift.

So, I did see some of your men leave the dorm premises in the middle of the night. It wasn't like they were tiptoeing towards the cafeteria to swipe beer from the fridge. They were *running* and *screaming*, Gestur. What they were running from, I have no idea. The camera was situated at a place where I couldn't see the intruder.

Did you not hear them screaming that night, Gestur? I realize the storms up on the glacier can get pretty loud at this time of year, but you must have heard *something*, right?

Keep me posted, all right?

All the best,
Hörður.

Date: 03/17/2026
Time: 09:15 a.m.
From: Hörður Bjarnason <hordur@alfaljos.is>
To: Gestur Hilmarsson <gestur@gverktakar.is>
Subject: Hello?
Gestur,

Why aren't you answering your phone? Why can't I get in touch with the rest of your crew? Did the telephone lines snap during yesterday's blizzard? Do you need Search and Rescue?

Look, I'm getting worried. We haven't heard anything from anyone for the last couple of days. The crew's families have been contacting us, seeking answers and I hate not being able to give them *something*. Anything, really, just a brief hello would suffice.

Please, reply.

All the best,
Hörður.

Date: 03/18/2026
Time: 00:02 a.m.
From: Gestur Hilmarsson <gestur@gverktakar.is>
To: Hörður Bjarnason <hordur@alfaljos.is>
Subject: She came

I can't believe it …

I must have been seeing things. Too tired from all this weird fucking shit happening here.

I haven't gotten proper sleep since Árný, the cafeteria chef, disappeared. Having no food prepared for you sucks. There was only canned corn, beans and pears left in the pantry and combining that sounds even more horrible than starving yourself to death.

Tension has been high among the few that remain …

No food and no sleep make Gestur something, something …

But why did she come?

She's not supposed to be here. She's not even supposed to be walking on this godforsaken earth!

She still came. She walked barefoot on the hardened ice, wearing nothing but the dress she was buried in. It had been her favorite dress. *My darling,* out there in the blistering storm.

Her voice called out to me. God, it felt like an arrow pierced my heart to hear it again. She asked me an impossible task: To come join her in the magma. It's where people like us belong, she told me.

I don't know if the veil between the two realms had thinned or if I had simply been hallucinating from inhaling all those toxic fumes from the magma, but I swear to God, she *looked* and *sounded* real to me.

You cannot imagine the terrible grief I went through after losing her from her battle with lung cancer. I almost gave up myself. Wanted to end it and join her. She had been my everything. But I couldn't. Chickened out. Reminded myself I had to take care of the kids.

I'm ashamed to admit I took a few steps outside into the blizzard. If I could have just one more moment with her, I would.

The sleet hitting my face woke me up. She was still there, beckoning me. Her face contorted with taunting glee. Her voice hollowed and sneered, calling me a coward.

I shut the door on her. I've said goodbye to her once. I'm not doing it again.

Her voice bounces on every wall, following me wherever I go …

I can still hear it. Listen …

Don't you hear it?

[Audio Attachment, 2MB: based on the audio attachment, editor was unable to discern anything aside from white noise]

Date: 03/19/2026
Time: 07:30 a.m.
From: Hörður Bjarnason <hordur@alfaljos.is>
To: Gestur Hilmarsson <gestur@gverktakar.is>
Subject: What is going on over there?

Gestur,

If this is your idea of a practical joke, it's not funny. If this is something your crew tends to do while away on an assignment, you need to stop it right now.

Were you drinking last night when you sent me that email? If you were, it's highly unprofessional of you. What a load of drivel. There was nothing on that audio clip, except for the wind sweeping across the speaker system. No voice whispering sweet nothings into my ear, whatsoever.

Also, Árný has gone as well?? You should have alerted me of this immediately instead of mentioning her in passing.

This is very unlike you, Gestur. I'm very concerned for your wellbeing as well as the wellbeing for the rest of your crew.

You've left me no choice. I've contacted the police as well as Search and Rescue and requested their help. Once the weather dies down, they'll be on their way to the facilities.

You better be sober when they arrive.

Regards,
Hörður.

Date: 03/21/2026
Time: 02:00 a.m.
From: Gestur Hilmarsson <gestur@gverktakar.is>
To: Hörður Bjarnason <hordur@alfaljos.is>
Subject: COME QUICK!!

I'm sorry, Hörður.

I don't know how else to start … I failed. No, I cracked under pressure. Yeah, I guess you could say that.

Thank you for alerting the police. I'm glad they're coming. They wouldn't have taken me seriously if I had called them myself.

I ... did something terrible.

Geiri ... Konráð ... all of them are dead.

I couldn't help it ...
I hadn't gotten any sleep since my wife appeared. She kept me awake with her incessant taunts. No amount of ear plugs or heavy metal music at the highest volume could drown her out. I couldn't hear anything else, not even when my crew stood in front of me mouthing something I couldn't understand.

Then somehow, she got inside. I saw her everywhere; she lurked in the main building, danced around the chairs in the cafeteria, slammed the doors in the cabins and even swayed on the steel lanes near the drills down below (see image attachment).

I was going crazy, but I persevered and managed to ignore the ghastly sights till I drank myself unconscious.

The last couple of days are a blur. I remember bits and pieces ...

Grabbing an emergency axe from the case in the hallway ...
Seeing her wretched face approaching me ... the voice I had loved drilling into my ears ...
Me, finally having had enough.
A good old-fashioned chase through the hallways. Screaming. Or was it laughter?
Blisters on my hands—muscles feeling taut from over-exertion—blood obscuring my vision—laughter.
So much laughter ... It didn't sound human at all. At least I had gotten rid of her face.

When I came to, I was standing in the warehouse. Mangled bodies, in various stages of decomposition, littered the concrete. Maggots writhed through pus-festered wounds. It was my missing crew.
I remember screaming till my throat grew hoarse and raw. Bile rushing from my esophagus and exiting violently on the floor. I scrambled out of the slaughterhouse and went searching for the others.

Security cameras told me they were down below where the drills were. Their cut-up bodies greeted me when I stepped on the narrow lane. Blood dripped through the grid, sizzling from the extensive heat.

I barely recognized Geiri and Konráð among the mutilated corpses. My hands still held on to the bloody axe. I hadn't noticed it till now.

Then something moved underneath the severed body limbs. Child sized and drenched in dark crimson they appeared obsidian. An oily hue slicked their narrowed eyes. Jagged rows of teeth chomped into the dead flesh. Sharp claws pierced through the limbs like clay. Scratches reverberated from the rocks. Tiny stones toppled from the cracks as more shapes grew bigger and more prominent, eager to join the feast.

LOOK, YOU HAVE TO HURRY!

I've locked myself in my office, but I know they're coming. Shit, Sævar and Leifur were right. I should have listened to them, but it's too late. They're gone. All of them … I'm the only one left … and they're coming for me!

No, wait …

WAS THAT BANGING ON THE DOOR??

I HEAR SCRATCHES!

FUCK, THOSE SHRIEKS! IT'S LIKE THEY'RE BURROWING INTO MY BRAIN!

IT'S THEM!!

OH, GOD, THE DOOR IS OPENINGROGJRGRIBRBIBRIBIB RIBRRIRRIRBIRRIRBIRRIBRIRRIRIRRIRIRBIGBRIBGIRBIRBRI BRIRRRRRRRRRIRRIRRRR

[Image Attachment, 25MB: Due to the grainy resolution, editor was unable to discern any kind of human shape in the image]

Tupperware Party

The time was perfect.

No kids in the way. None of those high shrieks that made anyone grind its teeth and wish they'd just drown in the summer pool. No one had time for that. The killer had made sure of it.

No, it was just the husband at home. Home from work where he expected the lovely housewife to greet him at the stairs with a can of beer and a sweet smile. Of course, the housewife had been taken care of. The killer had made extra sure of that.

The killer watched the husband grumble as he got himself something to eat from the refrigerator. Leftover chicken pot pie that he heated up in the microwave with less enthusiasm, judging from the frown squared on his face. He wouldn't take too long to eat; the killer had watched him long enough to know that. Afterwards he would go upstairs, play with himself in the bathroom with the help of the porn magazines he kept stashed underneath the unread cooking magazines. Again, that wouldn't take too long either, the killer surmised.

Once the husband retreated into the bedroom, the butterflies in the killer's stomach wreaked havoc. The time has come. Months of planning and everything had gone according to it. But the killer had to wait until the husband took his nightly walk into slumberland.

Not too long, now.

Snores gradually filled the master bedroom. The killer strode out of its hiding place from one of the kids' bedrooms, carrying a thick nylon thread. The husband slept on his back, like so many times the killer had watched him. The killer carefully positioned the husband's arms upwards, toward the bed's pillars. The husband moaned. The killer froze, its hands still cradling the husband's wrist. The killer stood still, heart lodged in its throat, until the husband smacked his lips and continued snoring. The killer breathed a sigh of relief and resumed fastening the husband's arms to the pillars with the nylon thread.

After checking the thread withstood a few strong tugs, the killer climbed on top of the husband and straddled him. The mere movement and weight below his midriff caused an erection, which the killer had anticipated. The husband gave another moan and roused, his eyelids flickering open. His face split into a surprised smile.

"Oh, this is nice. What's the occasion?"

The killer smiled and brandished its shiny new carving knife. "A surprise," the killer said.

The husband's eyes widened, and he opened his mouth to scream. The killer clamped a gloved hand on his mouth, stifling his shrieks, and ran the blade into his abdomen slowly. The husband's eyes bulged, his body tensing under the sheer pain. The killer extracted the knife in a slow motion, as if savoring the glee. Blood poured from the wound, staining the sheets. The killer let out a small giggle as it rammed the blade into the soft flesh, delightful shivers cascading in tune to the crimson waterfalls. The blood pooled underneath the husband, his complexion growing pale and sickly. The killer mounted off and slid the sheets from his legs, revealing the flaccid penis hidden within his boxers. The husband gurgled in pathetic whimpers.

The killer smiled once again. "A souvenir for the night."

The killer grabbed his penis and took deliberate time carving it off from his body. It reveled in the sinews snapping, the arteries exploding as it sawed it apart. Blood spurted into the husband's face just before he gave into the pain. His body slumped in the bed, droplets of blood pitter-pattering on the hardwood floor.

The killer took one look at the dismembered member and tossed it on the mutilated body. Blood covered the killer's whole features. It felt a vindictive pleasure smearing it across its body.

But it wasn't over.

In fact, the party had just begun.

Mid-August signaled the end of summer in various ways; the apple trees were ripe with juicy fruits; the breeze carried colder air; the neighborhood felt the absence of bird songs in the mornings and excitement bubbled over in children's stomachs for the new school year. Which, of course, added stress to the mothers who had to buy everything their children needed, including water bottles and lunch boxes.

Patricia's Tupperware party thankfully provided all those necessities and more, with bottles of chardonnay and finger food to entice the hesitant ones in the neighborhood.

An uncomfortable knot twisted Martha's gut. "I don't know about this," she said for the second time as she checked her makeup in the rearview mirror. "Are you sure we can't cancel at the last minute?"

Her friend and next-door neighbor, Denise, rolled her eyes. "No, that'd be really rude, you know that."

Martha sighed and rummaged through her purse for nicotine gum. Giving up smoking right in the middle of school preparations had been a really bad idea. She silently prayed to God to give her patience for this day as she stuffed three pieces of gum into her mouth.

Denise scoffed, chuckling. "Why are you so nervous, anyway? It's just a Tupperware party. If anything, it's an excuse to get hammered on a weekday."

Martha looked out the car window, at the picturesque white picket fenced, cornflower-painted two-story house a few yards ahead. "I just don't know what to expect from it. Especially since Patricia is throwing that party."

Denise shrugged, adding extra lipstick on her lips and fluffing her already voluminous beehive of a hair. "Whatever has got her panties up in a bunch is not our problem, you hear me?"

"But I don't like to be given the cold shoulder, not when I don't know what I did to deserve it," Martha whined, tossing the wad of gum out the window and stuffing a few more into her mouth.

Denise smirked. "Well, today you get the chance to ask her."

Martha stared wide-eyed in terror at her friend. "I could never do that. I'm horrible at confrontations."

Denise winked before stepping out of the car. "No wonder Stephen gets what he wants."

Martha blushed, spluttering incoherent rationalizations while the two of them grabbed a casserole and a three-bean dip from the passenger seats and set out for Patricia's house. Martha breathed in the crisp autumn air, savoring the alluring scent of the ripened apples growing in the front of Patricia's house. A drip of jealousy slithered down her throat like ooze. The patch of green on her lawn only managed to produce weeds. *I guess Patricia has more time sprucing things up when she's stuck at home all the time,* she thought, then immediately felt bad. She shouldn't judge others so quickly. People don't know what's going on behind the scenes.

Ah, there *was* a reason for Martha's knot. Minivans and hatchbacks lined the sidewalk leading to Patricia's house. Patricia had probably invited the whole neighborhood.

She turned to Denise. "Is Robin invited?"

Denise's mouth spread into a thin line. "As far as I know."

Martha cringed. "Well, *that's* going to be an awkward reunion, don't you think?"

Denise gave a stiff nod. "If everyone from the barbeque comes, then I'll be planting myself at the drinks table. As much as I love drama, I don´t need VIP seating for it."

Martha bit her lower lip, clutching the casserole tighter to her chest. "I just want to get this over with. Who knows, maybe someone will actually buy a punch bowl or a lunch box. Maybe we'll end up having a great time. It's been over three months since we all gathered together."

Denise patted Martha on the shoulder. "And you haven't even gotten your first drink yet. Love that optimism."

The pristine white door stood before them. Neither Martha nor Denise wanted to knock on it. Martha was sure that she'd get tomato paste smudged on the wood and that would raise a lot of eyebrows from the rest of the curious neighborhood.

"Are we just going to stand here?" Denise chuckled before rapping her knuckles on the door.

Hurried clacking of heels clicked behind the door and once it opened, the personification of glee appeared. Patricia Henderson wore her tightest dress, the fabric clinging to her curves and falling down to her ankles. Golden jewelry trapped her wrists, fingers and neck. Martha resisted the urge to shield her eyes as the evening sun glistened on them.

Deep-red lipstick painted Patricia's smiling lips. "Martha! Denise! I'm *so* happy you could come. Come on in, almost everyone is here."

Martha caught Denise's incredulous side-eye before they stepped through the threshold. They looked ridiculous compared to her, in their cardigans and mom jeans.

Thankfully, they weren't the only ones. The rest of the neighborhood shared a similar dress style. Nancy Carter, who lived three houses adjacent from Martha, arrived in her sweatpants and tried to conceal it by draping Patricia's couch pashmina over her legs.

Patricia's living room was like a cut-out from *Better Homes and Gardens;* white cushy sofas with purple and black cushions to make them pop; the carpets were so soft Martha wanted to slip out of her sneakers and curl her toes in them; Patricia's family smiled at the guests in every portrait, big and small, that adorned the beige-colored walls.

Martha's jealousy sizzled within. It was like Patricia was looking down at some of the women who had to work alongside their spouse to earn a decent living.

She spotted the table behind the sofa where bottles of chardonnay and pigs-in-blankets waited for them.

"Oh, you brought a tuna casserole? That's so sweet of you. I hope the girls will be hungry enough after my presentation," Patricia trilled.

Heat burned Martha's cheeks. She hurried over with her sad piece of a casserole and placed it behind the tray of scrumptious cheese and broccoli quiches. Denise made a beeline for the table as well, but only to have a tall drink.

A variety of colorful plastics littered the lawn table next to the armchair where Patricia stood, beaming at her guests. "Well, I think it's all right to get started, right, ladies?"

Martha sat down on the sofa adjacent to the hostess while Denise chose to stand near the drinks. As Patricia began her presentation with a brief history of the Tupperware products, Martha instantly regretted sitting so close, her mind taking her back to high school when she struggled to pay attention to the teacher's drone.

Even the way Patricia presented each colorful plastic bowl with a flourish, akin to a professional car salesman, wasn't enough to keep her interested. It was *plastic bowls*, for God's sake. Martha covered her yawn by ducking down in search of lip balm in her purse. *I could have wasted my evening taking care of the kids instead of this crap,* she thought miserably but made sure to keep her fake smile plastered on her face.

The doorbell chimed.

Some of the women jumped, as if caught napping and cleared their throats. Patricia froze, glitter-resin lunch box held tight in her hands. She stood like that for a moment, gazing straight at the front door.

"Aren't you going to answer it?" Denise asked, tipping the third glass of chardonnay in her gullet.

A shadow flickered across Patricia's eyes before she blinked and gave Denise the sweetest smile. "But of course. It just threw me off, the bell, you see?" She carefully placed the product back on the table and sauntered off to greet the latecomer.

Nancy let out a groan. "How much more of this are we gonna take?"

Erin West, whose son was in the same class as Martha's girl, rubbed her temples. "Not long, I hope. I'm getting a migraine from Patricia's shrill performance."

The women snickered, including Martha, though she felt bad about it at once.

"C'mon, you guys. She invited us over, gave us free food and expensive white wine. The least we can do is endure it and maybe buy a lunch box or two," she said to soothe her guilty conscience.

Nancy, Erin, Denise, and the rest made faces but eventually grumbled "yes" into either their drinks or plates of food. Heels clattering the hardwood floor which then muffled under the living room carpet announced the arrival of the new guest.

Martha turned to give Patricia an encouraging smile. It died on her lips, shriveling into a parted surprise. Denise's eyes widened and she nearly choked on the white wine.

Patricia led Robin Clove into the living room, her tittering voice gushing about how happy she was that she'd made it.

Robin didn't look as happy, with her hunched shoulders, hands shoved in her leather jacket and smoky eyes darting in every direction, registering that almost the entire neighborhood was present.

"Oh, hey, the gang is all here," Robin chuckled awkwardly.

"Yes, isn't it nice? We all haven't been together like this since …" Patricia's voice trailed off as her bright eyes glazed in thought.

A stone lodged itself in Martha's gut. She glanced at the women. All of them avoided looking at the hostess. They all knew the last time had been at the barbeque.

"Well, it doesn't matter. We're all here now. *That's* what matters," Patricia said with a giggle.

She beckoned Robin to the only seat available, right next to the products' table. Robin forced a grin as she eyed the cheap plastic household items. She remained silent, however, when she went for the seat.

Martha realized the air had changed—everyone seemed wide awake and alert. Denise hadn't even picked up a fourth glass as she stared rapt between Patricia and Robin.

"Now, where was I? Oh, right! These containers are to die for! They can store any food for a long period of time, are dishwasher safe and don't contain any crap that are harmful to our loved ones. Don't you use any containers for your leftovers, Robin?" Patricia directed her words at Robin while placing lilac-colored soup container onto her lap.

Robin startled. "Huh? Oh, yeah, I think so, though I don't cook much."

Patricia nodded and carried on, as if she hadn't heard Robin's reply. "Now, I know summer is almost over, but water bottles are essential in everyone's bags. These ones are so convenient because of the built-in straws, so you can just suck on them at any part of the day."

She handed Robin a pink water bottle. "Guzzling down any kind of liquid is *so* good, wouldn't you agree, Robin?"

A dull patch of red bloomed through Robin's makeup. "Yeah, s-sure."

Martha wanted to crawl under the sofa cushion or throw up. Anything to get away from the awkward cringefest happening before their very eyes. She glanced over to Denise, who was nowhere to be found. That cunning bitch, slipping out and leaving her alone in a disaster awaiting to happen. She felt so bad for Robin for being Patricia's unwilling sales assistant.

Patricia gave a hearty laugh and replaced the bottle back on the table. "Look at you blush, darling. Were you that red in the face while you were fucking my husband?"

Martha blinked. Had she misheard? Her eyes shot between Robin and Patricia. Patricia stood still, a smug smile playing on her lips as she leered down at the woman beside her. Robin got caught between chuckling and stammering, smoky eyes searching within the room for anyone to help her.

The neighborhood, however, had turned into a shocked court jury who'd been presented with a juicy piece of evidence. Evidence they had known about for a long time.

"How did you know?" Martha whispered.

Patricia scoffed. "I'm not that stupid, even though you treat me as such, Martha." She waved to a dragonfly fire alarm in the upper corner to her left. "We've got security cameras inside as well as outside in the backyard, in case you all forgot."

Robin blanched, clutching the armrest.

"That barbeque was supposed to create great memories, for us all to get along better. So, while I was busy being the best hostess in the neighborhood, I caught Mike and Robin going into the tool shed and spending an awful long time there." Patricia pointed at each and every woman in the room. "And you all saw it, yet you didn't have the courtesy to tell me. Some friends you are. But you—" she turned to Robin whose lips trembled. "Betraying my hospitality and violating my marriage is unforgivable."

Robin opened her mouth to speak. A scream from beyond the kitchen interrupted her attempt at making excuses.

Denise stumbled into the living room and clutched the back of the sofa. She stammered incoherently, pointing to the place she had been in the back.

Frowning, Martha got up and went to her friend. She probably wanted to apologize for throwing up in the closet or something. It wasn't the first time it had happened. She gently patted her back. "You okay, honey?"

Denise vehemently shook her head, face ghastly pale and eyes wide. "I went to look for the guest bathroom. I thought it was here on the first floor but I opened the door to the garage instead. I-I—" Denise's lips trembled, staring at Patricia.

Martha held down her scoff, though something else pierced her heart in dreadful pinpricks. "What is it?" she pressed.

Denise broke into hysteric sobs. "I just found Mike in the garage. He's *dead*!"

Patricia groaned and threw up her hands. "Thanks for blowing my surprise."

In such swiftness Martha didn't know Patricia possessed, she grabbed a carving knife from the table and plunged it deep between Robin's breasts. Blood sprayed from the wound as she extracted the blade, peppering the carpet with crimson droplets.

The women stared in stony disbelief. Robin gurgled, bloody bubbles popping from her mouth.

"Oh, that felt *good*," Patricia moaned and rammed the blood-soaked blade back in Robin's midriff, again and again until the leather jacket drowned in blood.

Screams tore through the living room. Feet scrambled on the squelching carpet, tripping and slipping. Patricia grabbed Erin by the hair and ran the knife across her throat, slicing the windpipe in a clean line. Blood gushed like a fountain, creating abstract art on the stark white sofa. Patricia shrieked with laughter when she tackled Nancy to the floor, slicing at her arms and leaving strands of skin hanging like curtains.

Martha went for the front door. Two of the women already banged on the door, crying hysterically.

"It's locked! We can't get out!"

Patricia had removed the door handle. She must have done it after Martha and Denise had come inside or after greeting Robin. Footsteps thundered toward the exit. Martha's heart pounded in her chest. Judging from the cameras and the whole setup, she knew Patricia had planned for this all along. No one was supposed to get out of here alive. She turned around and ran through the dining room and into the kitchen. The padlock on the backdoor looked brand new and hindered them to get out to safety. Another door presented itself to the left—the garage door.

Martha stormed inside and closed the door behind her. She turned around and gasped. Mike's corpse lay splayed on a pile of garbage bags, like the scum Patricia had deemed him to be. She had even carved the word "trash" across his forehead.

She took a wide berth away from the gruesome display of hatred and tried the small garage door. Another padlock blocked her path. She looked up and groaned. The automated garage door had been busted; no doubt done by Patricia. Martha needed a place to hide. Revulsion crawled up Martha's spine. Beggars couldn't be choosers, certainly not at this moment. She swallowed the bile and breathed through her mouth as she slid underneath Mike's cold corpse.

Minutes passed, yet Martha felt like she's spent a lifetime in a makeshift grave. She couldn't stay hidden forever. One way or another, Patricia would find her and kill her. Images of her children flashed before her mind.

No.

Her children would *not* grow up motherless. Martha scanned the garage. It had all of Mike's presence there and none of Patricia's; the SUV parked in the middle; the fishing gear stashed in the corner; hunting gear marked in boxes above the worktable.

Martha stared. Determination surged through her veins. She crawled out of the garbage heap, stalked over to the worktable, and climbed atop it.

"Please, be there. Be like my stupid husband and leave it untouched but ready," she whispered as she rummaged through the clothes inside the boxes. Her frantic fingers touched long, cold metal. She inadvertently let out a relieved laugh. "Be ready, you bitch."

Martha took a deep breath, holding the shotgun tight to her chest. She carefully opened the garage door and tiptoed to the living room.

Patricia's pristine home had transformed into a slaughterhouse. The iron stench of blood hung heavy in the air. Severed limbs scattered the slick hardwood floor. All of them had the word "traitor" carved crudely into their flesh. Patricia sat in the middle of the living room coffee table, straddling a limp Denise, and giggling as she carved the insignia on Denise's cheeks.

Martha pushed the need to vomit back into the void. She raised the shotgun with trembling arms.

"Hey, Patricia," she called.

Patricia looked up, dazed from her euphoria. Her eyes widened.

"Your party sucked." Martha cocked the gun, aimed and pulled the trigger.

Patricia's head exploded like a ripe melon. Chunks of skull fragments, blood and gray matter smeared the curtains, sparing the window from the gore. Patricia's body slid off Denise and thumped on the carpet.

Martha threw the gun aside, clasping her twitchy fingers in her hands. It was over. She let the tears flow. Her knees buckled and her butt hit against something hard on the floor. One of the Tupperware containers.

She glanced at the massacre surrounding her. They had all been her friends and Patricia had desecrated their corpses in such a heinous way. She couldn't leave them like that. She grabbed all the scattered containers and spent the evening collecting the dismembered fingers, hands, and feet in the bowls. She prayed as she arranged the bodies in sleeping positions until the police arrived. Up on the wall, she caught the dragonfly fire alarm in the corner of her eye.

Well, at least the surveillance cameras were useful for something.

HELL OF A RIDE

rumpled up drawings underneath the coffee table. Plushies strewn around the living room. A stiffness built up in Sarah's neck. Tommy is such a mess. She bent down to pick up one of the stuffed animals. It felt cold and wet to the touch. Frowning, she looked down. The floor was soaked in water. It pulled up to her ankles, as if the sea was beckoning. Sarah looked toward the bathroom. Water gushed out from the door. The wave slammed Sarah onto the coffee table. Something slid through the sodden carpet. Dark hair, sleeked down, obscuring the eyes. The small chest not moving. The lips blue. Absence of bubbles. Trembling, Sarah pushed the hair away. Hollow eyes met hers.

Sarah's eyes snapped open and she gasped. For a moment, she had no idea where she was. The back of cabin seats met her on the front. A small, condensed window hung to her left. A flight attendant pushed a wagon full of merchandise to her right. She blinked. She thought she was still in that apartment, gazing down at Tommy's lifeless body. Her heart pounded.

"Hey, you okay?" Laura pressed her hand on Sarah's arm.

Sarah took a deep, shuddering breath to calm her nerves before nodding. "Yeah, I'm fine. Just had a bad dream."

Laura's brows furrowed. "You're still having them? It's been over a year."

Sarah's lower lip trembled. A year. Has it been that long? She should have moved on by now. But she couldn't. Like her guilt, her foster son still haunted her dreams. He festered like unwanted tumor. She didn't want to linger on that dream. She turned to the left and rested her forehead on the cool glass.

The plane window offered an unobstructed view of a barren wasteland. Lava and black sand stretched over for miles. Sarah frowned.

"Where are the horses?"

Laura snorted as she put down her in-flight magazine. "It's not like we're going to Japan. According to this magazine, the population of Iceland is only three hundred and fifty thousand. They can't quite cover the entire island."

"Horses?"

"No, silly! People. You know, like all those hot, healthy guys I need to get you acquainted with? To get over Ryan?"

Sarah sighed and propped her hand under her chin. She was more excited of the prospect of riding horses than the pursuit of romance. "Oh, right. But when you told me we'd have an adventure in Iceland I just kind of expected it to be more, I don't know, magical."

Laura waved a dismissive hand. "We're just landing. Believe me, the magic will strike when we go into the city."

Sarah hoped so. Growing up in Oregon, she had been surrounded by trees. So vibrant and green. So … alive. A twinge tugged her gut. She looked out the window again. If that trip was based on first impressions, Sarah felt the country needed to step up its game. The grey lava reminded her of emptiness. She heaved a great sigh.

The drive into Reykjavík lifted Sarah's brooding mood somewhat. The cairn-scattered marsh from the airport transformed into colorful buildings nestling beneath mountains in the distance.

"Look at those skyscrapers! They're so small and cute!" Laura chirped as she pointed at a tall glass building near one of the miniscule shopping malls.

Sarah peeled away from her phone. She had been scrolling through the photos on her Instagram. Her account still preserved memories of her time with Ryan. With Tommy. She had been meaning to delete them after the funeral but couldn't bring herself to do it. She peered through the passenger window. She scoffed. She wouldn't have called those attempts skyscrapers. They were different, though. Reykjavík wasn't as crowded as New York and she was surprised to see no subway stations or trains along the road. Icelanders seemed to travel only by cars or via the yellow-orange buses she kept spotting. She was glad that Laura had rented a car for the two of them. Despite Sarah's dislike toward the desolate environment, she craved isolation. Hypocritical, but she felt like she didn't quite belong to the human race.

The apartment they booked was just as cozy and cute as the picturesque capital. The white painted walls reminded Sarah of the snow that covered the surrounding mountains. The furniture, however, was bright and warm but minimal. Scandinavian style according to the magazine Sarah skimmed through on the flight. A small armchair and a red sofa fit to room two or three people surrounded an oak coffee table. The bedrooms were small but cozy and well-heated. Sarah shivered in appreciation as a frosty wind banged on the windows and seeped in through lax seals.

"So, are we ready for some exploring?" Laura dropped her suitcase on the bed.

Sarah glanced at the simple white clock on the wall, then at the window where the wind moaned a ghoulish dirge. It was only mid-afternoon, yet the sun had already slipped beneath the mountains, beckoning the night to take its place. Sarah yawned. It had been a six-hour flight. She wanted nothing more than to curl up on the sofa and let the TV anesthetize her.

However, Laura's excitement bewitched her. Weather never bothered her. Not when they had sought shelter underneath a tree during a drenching monsoon in Thailand. Not when they had been parched and sunbaked through their trek in blistering Nevada. The winter gale outside was probably nothing more than a cool breeze to Laura. Sarah suppressed a sigh. "Sure. Where do you want to go?"

Laura's eyes gleamed as she pointed out the window, at the bizarre church pyre at the top of the capital's hill. "Let's go look at the view from the top of Hallgrímskirkja Church! And then, there's this ice-cream made from ryebread that I´ve been dying to try!"

The whirlwind named Laura gusted them up into a bevy of activities. From whale watching near Faxaflói bay—where Sarah puked her breakfast—to eating puffin meat for the first time. Laura ate it all with gusto while Sarah managed only a couple of bites before turning a shade of green.

Strange food aside, Icelanders welcomed the pair with open arms. That went double when the bars and clubs opened. Reykjavík downtown beckoned with bright lights and alluring drinks. Music, American and Icelandic, boomed through the crowded streets. A throng of drunk people pressed forward, vying for a spot in the loudest club. Sarah had been a freshman in college when she last danced and drank till four in the morning.

Vegan lattes in the snug cat cafe combatted the next day's blinding hangovers. That and therapeutic kitty cuddles with the feline denizens that practically owned the place.

But hangovers aside, Sarah finally felt at ease—more at ease than she had in ages—the excruciating pain of traumatic memories fleeting as the snow flurries.

Until the cold crept back in, icy fingers clutching around her heart.

As the ice cubes rattled at the bottom of her fourth *Sushi Social* cocktail, Sarah blubbered in the ear of the hot, healthy guy who had purchased the rhubarb cocktail for her. At first, she had balked at the concept of rhubarb in a mojito, but the damned gardens around here seemed to fester with the stuff. After a few of the sweet drinks, though, all Sarah could talk about was Ryan. How he'd left her a few months after the accident. Left her right when she needed him most.

She scowled into her drink. The liquid swirled in a tiny maelstrom until it began taking shape. Dark hair clinging to a sodden, pale face. Water spilling out of blue lips. Sarah gasped and threw the glass on the floor. *Tommy.* Her ranting dissolved, right along with any interest from Mr. Hot-n-Healthy, as her body racked with hysterical sobs. Laura disengaged from her own potential one-night stand to drag a blubbering Sarah all the way back to the apartment where she spent hours consoling her.

The morning after was hazy.

Sarah stumbled out of bed, clutching her phone. A killer headache pounded her skull.

"Morning," Laura sat in the kitchen and flipped through the Fréttablaðið, one of Iceland's newspaper. She pretended not to see her.

Sarah winced at her icy tone. She shuffled to the sink and poured herself a glass of water.

When Sarah sat down opposite her, Laura pushed a plate of pastry to her. "Care for a rhubarb pastry?"

Foggy memories of last night stirred in her head. Of a weird rhubarb cocktail. And then what followed after guzzling four of those cocktails. Sarah's cheeks reddened.

"I'm sorry." She dipped her chin almost to her chest.

Laura shrugged. "It's fine."

It definitely wasn't. Sarah had ruined their night-out. She couldn't bear to have her friend be pissed off at her for the rest of the trip.

"No, I made a complete fool of myself. How can I make it up to you?"

A wicked grin curled up Laura's lips. She tore a page from the newspaper and placed it above the pastry. "I've got a few things in mind."

Sarah glanced down. On the bottom of the page were advertisements for two different walking tours through Reykjavík's streets—one that involved more Icelandic food, which Sarah's stomach wasn't keen on. The other featured a "walk among elves" in Hafnarfjörður, the supposed town of elves and hidden people. Sarah bit the inside of her cheek. That was going to be a *long* day.

Supernatural hooey didn't particularly fascinate Sarah—she was the type that needed evidence shoved into her face—but Laura lapped it all up. Her best friend walked beside their guide, Álfheiður, and listened intently to every story and snapped photos of every rock that was supposed to be a home of the elves.

"But what about waters?" Laura asked as they passed by a small lake in central Hafnarfjörður. "Do elves live there as well?"

Álfheiður beamed. "Some do, but the lakes usually are the homes to Sæneyti, Laxamóðir and Nykur, the many of our Icelandic monsters."

Laura's eyes bulged in enthusiasm. "Monsters? Wait, you mean they actually existed here?"

Álfheiður nodded. "We have stories of them existing since the settlement of Iceland. There is a tale of Nykur originating from the Book of Settlement, for example."

Laura sidled closer to the guide and looped her arms with hers, stars in her thirsty eyes. "Tell me more."

Sarah rolled her eyes and wrapped her scarf closer around her neck. Good old Laura. Whenever they went to a new place, she *had* to absorb all the native folklore and myths. She probably didn't even feel how tired her feet should be or how the wind bit at every exposed surface. Tuning out the drivel, Sarah dug out her phone from her pocket. No message from her parents. Not even "how are you holding up?"

"I'd love to see a real monster," Laura gushed.

Sarah snorted.

Álfheiður raised one curious eyebrow at her, then turned back to Laura.

"But would you know a true monster if you saw one?" she asked.

A furrow deepened between Sarah's brows.

"Of course, I would!" Laura declared. "Everyone knows that monsters are ugly, ferocious things."

Álfheiður clucked her tongue and wagged her finger. "Not our monsters. Take Nykur, for example. Just a regular Icelandic horse. Thing is, a lot of drownings have been attributed to Nykur."

"Why's that?" Sarah asked. She thought of the horses in Laura's picture, with their placid horsey grins.

Laura nodded too, eager to hear Álfheiður's explanation.

"Well, if you sat on Nykur's back and tried to ride him, he would ride you toward a lake, dragging you to the depths, and drown you. Some people used to think that Nykur was the devil in disguise."

Laura let out a dramatic gasp, completely immersed in the story.

"The monsters are not always bad. Sæneyti, for example, looks like a cow and it was thought fortunate if farmers got one to mate with their own cows. And Bjarndýrakóngurinn, a beast that looks like a polar bear but with a glowing gold stone on his head, would be your savior if you got lost in a blizzard." Álfheiður pulled out a picture book from her backpack and showed the group photos of the beasts.

Laura stood on her toes to get a better look, tripped on a rock and almost stumbled into the lake herself.

Álfheiður caught her, chuckling. "Be careful. You don't want Nykur to find you."

They both laughed as the tour continued. Sarah glanced at the lake. Her reflection glittered against the frozen surface. She had a hard time believing a creature could emerge from a place like that. It was all just superstition and urban legends. Seeing was believing. The wind blew snow in her eyes. Spluttering, she cast her eyes downward again. Tommy looked up at her from beneath the ice. Eyes dull and lifeless. Bubbles erupting from his mouth.

Gasping, she staggered backwards. Her heels caught an uneven patch of the sidewalk. Curious tour-goers stared at her in bewilderment, stopping in their tracks to ogle her.

"Laura!" Sarah reeled back from the image, scrambling away from the lake. As her came running, she reached out to her.

The guilt wouldn't even allow her to suffer through a damn walking tour.

Their little trip was almost coming to an end. The only thing left was the distracting adventure Sarah had been looking forward to since they left New York.

The air around her and Laura, however, had been stiff and awkward since they had to leave in the middle of the walking tour.

"I'm sorry about what happened," Sarah began. She fiddled with a loose seam on the sleeve of her sweater.

Laura said nothing, only gripped the steering wheel tighter.

"I'm just still trying to adjust. Clearly, it's not working." Sarah gave a weak chuckle. She couldn't tell if the iciness she felt was from the outside or Laura.

"Are you taking the medications the doctor prescribed you?" Laura glanced from the road to Sarah.

Sarah clenched her hands, nails digging into her palms. Her heart quickened a few pulses. "No, I get nauseous from them."

Laura heaved a deep sigh. "No wonder your outbursts are getting more frequent. Listen to me, the pills are supposed to help you. The doctor prescribed them because you didn't want to go to therapy and talk about the accident. You don't talk to anyone about it. Not even me, and I'm supposed to be your best friend."

Sarah turned away from the hurt in Laura's face. She wanted to talk to her about it. But cold fear had her tongue frozen. What if Laura was repulsed by what had happened? What if she broke ties? She'd be completely alone. Sarah knew she wouldn't be able to handle that.

"Someday, I promise." Even though her hand was clammy, Sarah put hers on Laura's.

Though a small smile tugged at Laura's lips, she slightly moved her hand away. "Okay, but you better promise me that you'll take the meds when we get back home."

Sarah nodded and crossed her chest with her finger. "Cross my heart."

The remaining unspoken words of that familiar phrase echoed in Sarah's head.

In Tommy's voice.

The road trip to the west of Iceland brought them to a fortress of snowy mountains. Even Sarah had to admit that the scenery became more hauntingly beautiful as they approached Snæfellsnes peninsula. It felt lonely and cold, long nights claiming much of the day, but Sarah felt certain nature would dethrone the dark nights come spring. Sarah longed for the light.

Winter's icy fingers held tight on its reign, blasting the car with swift, northern gales.

Unease coiled within Sarah's stomach. "Do you think it'll be all right to go horseback riding in this weather?"

Laura shrugged. "You know how the weather has been here. Changes every fifteen minutes. Sunshine and daisies in the morning. Snot-freezing cold by noon."

"I hope so," Sarah mumbled, knowing firsthand how quickly life could turn on a dime. She stared out the window, watching the few birch trees bend to the unforgiving wind.

"Look, I can see the glacier up ahead!" Laura's eyes lit up. A big smile spread across her face.

Sarah leaned forward in her seat. It didn't really look like a glacier. Not a humongous block of ice that is continually moving at a snail's pace. Instead it was just a broad, cone-shaped mountain covered in greyish ice at the bottom. It reminded her more of Mt. Fuji in Japan.

"Why did you want to ride here again? We could have gone to any place near Reykjavík for horses. I saw them at almost every vacant yard of grass."

Laura's eyes gleamed. "You know how much I love Jules Verne. This glacier, Snæfellsnesjökull glacier, is in *A Journey to the Center of the Earth*, my favorite story. It serves as the gateway to the Earth's core. Going there has been on my bucket list forever. I'm so happy that I'm finally here."

Laura's infectious smile spread to Sarah's own lips. "Thanks for letting me be a part of it."

Laura stroked Sarah's arm, beaming. "Anytime, honey."

The horse-riding experience was near Hellnar, a small fishing village beneath the Snæfellsnesjökull ice cap. Laura and Sarah were not the only ones excited to ride the adorable Icelandic horses. A whole British family of four and a German couple lined up in front of the small, wooden cabin, waiting for the guide to show them their animal companion for the day.

The guide arrived, miniature horses in tow. Their manes billowed in the wind. Their colorful coats glistened in the sun which had decided to peek from behind the dismal gray snow clouds. While smaller than the horses Sarah was used to, their muscles rippled taut and ready.

"Good day to you all," The guide, a stocky man covered in auburn beard and wearing a thick parka, said. "I'm glad you found the place all right. Guess I won't have to call Search and Rescue."

Laura chuckled along with the tourists.

Sarah frowned. "Does that happen often?"

The guide waved a dismissive hand. "Only if you underestimate the weather here and what a real monster it can be. Glad you all are the sensible ones."

His quip earned him another laugh from the group. He introduced himself as Bjarki and then went ahead distributing the horses with the help of his family who had hung back.

Bjarki's young daughter came over to Sarah. She pulled along a horse with a grey coat and a long, black mane.

"Hi, I'm Margrét. You get the honor of riding Reykur, the newest of our four-legged family," she said brightly as she handed Sarah the reins.

Sarah reached out a hand, hesitated a bit before gently touching the horse's neck. Feeling his muscles stiffen, as if ready to run, gave Sarah pleasant chills. This was familiar territory, the heady scent already bringing her back to her youth. She inhaled and a big smile split her face. "What does Reykur mean?"

"It means smoke. Fits his color, don't you think?" Margrét said as she tightened the saddle.

Sarah stroked Reykur's mane away from his dark eyes. His nostrils flared but he kept his head bowed. Wary.

"Don't worry. You've nothing to fear."

The nightmares melted away with the sun. Instead, Sara drank in the dream. The horse. The scenery. The company. Everything clicked.

She inhaled the crisp winter air and reveled in the moment. She loved how her butt bumped on the saddle as Reykur trotted on the black sand at the beginning of their ride. The ocean to their right teased at their feet, the waves growing ever closer with each pull. But they were safe. The tide was low, and they were moving away from the beach. The group's destination was the base of the Snæfellsnesjökull glacier where they would go as near to the ice as the conditions allowed.

The rest of the group rode in an inverted vee, like a flock of migrating Arctic terns, listening to Bjarki's stories of west Iceland. His words fell mute to Sarah. She listened only to the wind singing in her ears as it whipped her hair; to the labored snort of her mount beneath her. That was all that mattered now.

Something cold and wet touched her cheek. Frowning, she looked up. Dark clouds blocked out the late afternoon sun. Tiny snowflakes drifted through the air. The wind gained sudden strength.

Sarah groaned.

"Thomas, don't fall back!" A British-tinged voice, strident and wavering, called.

Sarah's breath hitched. She nearly chocked up on the reins. That little boy's name was Thomas? As in Tommy?

She had paid no attention to the family of four when they had first arrived. Now, her gaze fixated on the boy. Dark hair, like Tommy. A sweet smile, like Tommy. Grief and guilt once again grabbed her and squeezed out life-giving air from her lungs.

She pulled on the reins and Reykur stumbled to a stop. He tossed his head in confusion. Sarah buried her face in his mane and suppressed her sobs.

Sleet drilled her face and parka. The wind, which moments ago had whispered promises of freedom in her ear, now howled admonishment from all directions. She glanced up. Panic choked her.

Blinding snow swallowed her sight. She saw nothing of the coast, the mountains. She couldn't even see tracks in front of her.

"Laura!" Sarah shouted.

The screeching cyclone drowned out her calls.

Sarah turned Reykur around, though in which direction, Sarah couldn't say with any degree of certainty. The horse's nostrils flared against the gusts, warm puffs of air escaping from his nose.

"You know the way back, don't you?" Declaration or plea, Sarah wasn't sure. She patted the horse's neck.

His ears flicked back and forth before he let out a neigh.

Sarah's memory dredged up a fact from her childhood. Horses typically neighed when they're separated from their team. If the group was close, the other horses would whinny in return.

Sarah listened. She huddled close to Reykur's neck. Reykur curled his upper lip as his sides heaved before neighing again.

Something screeched in a high, unearthly tone.

Sarah's gloved hands flew to her ears. Goosebumps prickled her skin.

Reykur reared on his hind legs and dumped Sarah from her saddle. She fell hard on her side. Pain surged throughout her being. Coughs racked her body as she gasped to replace the air that had been knocked from her lungs.

"Reykur!" She rasped as she watched the horse rear for the second time and dash off into the blinding storm.

Sarah stumbled to her feet, limping after the dissolving, retreating form of the horse. Her heart lodged in her throat. The pound of blood thrummed in her ears, blocking all other sound.

"Reykur!" She screamed into the blizzard. "Laura!" She repeated the cries till her voice ran rough.

The angry wind threw her own voice back at her. She was alone. Trapped within a raging tempest. Not that there was anyone to miss her. Cold reality sunk in. Not anymore.

No. Sarah gave a sudden shake against the cold. There was Laura. Laura who had always been there for her. Laura who was probably worried sick right now.

Sarah's jaw set. She steeled herself against the cold and used every ounce of energy to lift her right foot up and ahead. The pain sent electric shocks into her every limb. She gritted her teeth and concentrated on putting the next foot in front of her, and then the next, trying to shield her eyes from the sleet.

Thirty minutes, an hour, who knew how much later, Sarah spotted something big ahead of her. Her heart quickened. She squinted. Something grey with black hair contrasted starkly against the white snow.

Reykur. Relief flooded her. She trudged through the drift faster than her tired body wanted. Her feet ached from blisters, but she didn't stop until she could touch the grey coat.

The horse shielded his face from the biting gale, but it was definitely her four-legged companion.

"I'm so glad you stayed," Sarah wailed as she collapsed near his body, panting.

She wasted no time and climbed up on him. Bjarki's daughter had been lax tightening the saddle straps. The horse must have thrown it when he got spooked. Sarah linked her finger in Reykur's mane and threw her right leg over. Bareback it was.

"Come on, boy. Let's go back." She stroked his mane while squeezing her knees into his ribs.

He flicked his ears forward before getting lazily to his feet.

The fear felt bearable now that she wasn't alone. Bitter cold, however, seeped through her clothes. Shivering, she leaned forward and hugged the horse, trying to absorb some of his heat. No warmth radiated from his grey coat. Had he been too long outside? She remembered how Margrét had mentioned that he was a new addition to their horse family. Perhaps he hadn't yet acclimated to the wildly changing elements of the Icelandic weather.

She heard a sound in the distance. A voice. Calling her name.

Sarah's spirit soared. It was Laura. They were searching for her.

She opened her mouth to call back, but her words choked when the horse took a sharp turn to the left—away from Laura's frantic shouts.

"What are you doing? Home is to the right." Sarah gently pulled on his mane.

The horse shook his head, as if he understood her but willfully ignored it.

The blizzard around them began to diminish. Details began to come into focus. Sarah noticed they were approaching a frozen lake.

"You're going the wrong way. Turn around." She tugged harder, but a sliver of uncertainty weakened her grip ever so slightly.

The horse kept walking, his forward pace more determined than her tugs.

"What's the matter with you? Look where you're going, dammit!" Sarah groped the mane around his long face, feeling for his eyes on the sides.

The hide was smooth … and bare.

The blood in her veins froze. How was that possible?

Her gloved fingers inched closer to his forehead, sliding under the fetlock. They brushed the eyelid—

—of a single eye.

Sarah's heart pounded against her ribcage, thudding to get out. This wasn't Reykur. What the hell was it?

"What are you?" Her words barely escaped her lips.

The horse—or whatever it was—snorted.

Sarah could have sworn she heard it say "Nykur."

The name niggled a memory, but Sarah couldn't place it. All she knew for certain was she wanted off, off whatever the hell it called itself.

She tried swinging her leg. Nothing happened. She grabbed at her thigh and pulled. Nothing. It was stuck like glue.

Sarah whimpered as she pulled and pulled, clawing at the denim of her jeans. She tore a piece off, but her leg remained rigid against the grey coat.

The lake became more prominent—more imminent. The ice sparkled alluringly.

Laura's voice drifted on the swirling wind. Her desperate calls triggered something …

What that elf-guide talked about during the walking tour. About the horse-like water creature that dragged unwitting people into lakes … and drowned them.

Her blood slurried in her veins.

"No, no. Please don't take me. I don't deserve it." Sarah sobbed as she pounded futilely on the Nykur's neck.

The Nykur raised his head and neighed. A smug laugh to Sarah's ears. He tossed his head forward.

Sarah followed his gaze. She blinked rapidly.

Tommy, her Tommy, stood on the lake, eyes hollow and clothes drenched in water.

Sarah's heart almost stopped. It was the first time she had seen the poor boy so *solid*. Her memory had diminished him to a transparent ghost. A ghost that haunted her day after day.

Now, he raised a hand to her, beckoning her.

Sarah's shoulders quaked. It came to this. All because of a quick smoke and social media check out on the balcony. For leaving the water running. For not watching over a curious little boy.

The ice on the lake dissolved at the Nykur's touch.

Sarah gasped the second her shoes submerged. Instead of cold, her feet were on fire. Gooseflesh enveloped her entire body as the Nykur took them deeper into the water. Fitting, she thought. An eye for an eye. This was her hell. Nykur was her harbinger. Her own Charon.

Needles stabbed her face at last. Bubbles erupted from her mouth as she gasped her last. As they faded, Tommy came closer. His dimpled smile was distorted through the murky water. As he wrapped his swollen arms around Sarah in a final embrace, she heard muffled cries coming from the surface.

She could see Laura's distorted image through the rippling water, searching, calling.

Sarah's tears mingled with the water as Tommy and the Nykur dragged her to the depths.

ALL YOU CAN DRINK BUFFET

I'm going to die if I keep this up.

Ben rubbed his eyes. He'd been staring at his computer screen for five hour straight. He was used to working late back home in the States, but it was nothing compared to the work environment in Japan. He should have prepared himself for the cultural difference, but when his company had advertised a job exchange with a similar one in Japan, he'd jumped at the chance because when would he ever get an opportunity like that? Prior to moving, he had heard about the Japanese diligence and the importance of teamwork, but hearing about it was completely different than *actually* experiencing it.

Ben looked around the cramped box that was the office. His Japanese coworkers were utterly silent as they worked, only stopping to go to the bathroom. No chit-chat, no snacks on their desks, not even making small talk by the water cooler. They were all male, all older than him and each wore the same suit and similar glasses. It was like a mirror had been placed at each desk, the same person typing away on the keyboard reflecting on the surface, mimicking the exact same move at the exact same time. It was eerily fascinating and yet it was something that Ben couldn't wrap his head around, even after being in the company for a few weeks now. He shrugged it off as an example of culture shock and resumed his work. His department took care of tax forms from other departments of the company and they were instructed to double-check the forms, to see if there were any errors. They'd received over three hundred forms which meant they were forced to stay in the office until they finished every single file. He needed to finish his task or he'd be stuck in the office all night. Not an enjoyable event for a young adult in an exciting country.

His tired eyes darted to the left, where Ogawa, his desk buddy—a young man fresh out of university and just as new to the environment as Ben was—was going over a tax form that had been faxed over. It hadn't occurred to him until now that he and Ogawa were the only people in their twenties in the office, perhaps even in the entire department. Maybe this line of work wasn't appealing to a lot of Japanese youths?

"You about done?" he asked Ogawa in simple Japanese that he'd learned by watching anime.

Ogawa, his eyes not straying from the fax paper, nodded. "I don't know about you, but I need something to take the edge off afterwards. I hope we can go to a *nomihodai*."

Ben raised an eyebrow. "What's that?"

Ogawa grinned. "There are restaurants all over Japan that offer all-you-can-drink buffets. It's awesome. You just pay for the hour and you can drink as much as you want."

Ben liked that concept, but he wasn't particularly keen on trying it out in the middle of the work week. He'd have to remember to take his expat pals to such a place during the weekend. "Is it a common thing you do?"

Ogawa nodded enthusiastically. "We usually do it after work. Best thing about it, you get a chance to bond more with the coworkers there."

Ben glanced over the group of middle-aged men in the office. He wasn't sure if they had anything in common, but he was always willing to make small talk. He was an American, after all.

As the hours ticked by and no one seemed to be finishing their work, Ben realized he was experiencing Japan's infamous overtime, where *salarymen* spent an abnormal amount of time at their work place, working as a team to finish what had to be done for the day.

Ben glanced at the clock above Mr. Hisashi's desk. It was nearing midnight. His eyes burned from exhaustion. He was on his last file. He cracked his knuckles and punched in the last numbers with an audible sigh. "All done," he said in broken Japanese, a tired smile spreading across his lips.

He turned to Ogawa, and saw he'd finished as well. Ogawa gave him a thumbs-up before shuffling the fax papers into a neat pile on his desk.

"Well done, everyone," Mr. Hisashi said. His desk was in front of the other ones, establishing the hidden hierarchy within the department. "I'm sure the departments will be happy with the results tomorrow."

Ben stifled a yawn as he got up and put on his suit jacket. It was the same gray color as the other coworkers were wearing, but due to his blond hair and blue eyes, he still felt like he stuck out like a sore thumb. Nonetheless, he was relieved to finally go home to his small, studio apartment where the soft duvet on his bed seduced him with six hours of sleep. "All right, thanks for today and I'll see you all tomorrow," he said, bowed, and took a step toward the door.

"Where are you going, Ben?" Mr. Hisashi asked, bewildered.

Ben turned around. Mr. Hisashi, Ogawa, and the other six coworkers all stared at him incredulously, like they'd caught him red-handed stealing office supplies.

Unease crept up Ben's spine. "Oh, I thought we were done for the day, so I'm going home?"

Mr. Hisashi chuckled as he smoothed the comb-over on his head. He wagged his finger playfully. "Not before going out for drinks with us. We need to celebrate."

Ben's stomach soured. He was in no mood for drinks. He just wanted to get some much needed rest. He opened his mouth to decline, but caught the silent despair exuding from Ogawa, a plea to not abandon him. Ben shook his head. "Not tonight, thanks. Perhaps some other time."

The benign smile on Mr. Hisashi's face vanished. His kind, understanding eyes grew dark and bulgy as he approached Ben. "Excuse me? You're not going to join us for a *nomikai?*" His usual jovial voice was low and gravely, like an animal tensing for an attack.

Ben remembered vaguely an expat named Chris had told him that no matter what, he could *not* decline an invitation for a *nomikai* because it would be like refusing a request from a senior employer. Nothing was to disrupt the work balance, even after work hours. It was considered impolite and impractical to go against it. It could even result in a crack in the group mentality. Ben imagined himself being socially shunned, which was a death sentence when living in another country with values and culture different than what he was used to.

Cold sweat dripped from under his armpits. Chuckling nervously, Ben cleared his throat. "No, of course I am! I was just kidding."

Color came back to Ogawa's cheeks. Tension seemed to melt from his shoulders as Mr. Hisashi's old-man features returned to exuberant joy. The supervisor clapped his hands together. "Excellent, you're going to love our little gathering spot. It's got a lot of various alcohol to choose from. It will be a blast!"

Ben plastered a polite smile on his face and bowed again as Mr. Hisashi walked past him, with the rest of the older coworkers in tow. His stomach rumbled. Filling it up with drinks would have to do. He had to represent the best of the company, so there was *no way in hell* he'd disappoint his supervisor.

The loud noise coming from other drunk patrons in the next room cranked up Ben's tension headache that had begun plaguing him the minute he stepped inside the crowded restaurant. Ben wasn't used to eateries like that, where a waitress ushered people into small, cramped rooms. Inside was a long, narrow table in the middle of the room, with cushions lining each side. No chairs were in sight, whatsoever. Ben and the others would have to sit very closely together while Mr. Hisashi took it upon himself to order beer and whiskey for everyone on the small order pad that was glued on the wall behind him.

"So, how do you like Japan so far?" Mr. Hisashi asked, after putting the orders in and watching Ben, Ogawa, and the other coworkers settle themselves on the thin cushions.

The sudden question startled Ben. Should he be honest and say how much the cultural inconveniences were piling up in his head? He hated, for example, that only a few stores accepted cards and if he was short on cash, he was forced to walk 3 miles to the nearest 7/11 ATM that took his foreign card. He also wasn't a fan of the masks some people wore while in his presence. They would smile at him at first, but the second he turned away, they would whisper something about his foreigness; the size of his nose, his BO or how improper he could be. Of course, he could never voice this out to anyone except other expats who shared similar experiences, but Ben only met with them once a month and it got exhausting to complain about culture shock every time they got together.

"Oh, it's great," Ben hurried to say, swallowing the resentment that had begun building in his core. He was here to make progress, to get ahead. If that meant sucking up to the boss and lie about his feelings, so be it. He would not be the nail that stuck out.

Mr. Hisashi gave him an approving smile, patting him on the shoulder. "That's good. Work can be hard, but that just means we can play harder."

As if on cue, the drink orders came through the doors and soon the room competed with the other rooms in terms of rowdiness. Ben's other coworkers took turns pouring *sake* into Mr. Hisashi's small cup while the supervisor himself encouraged them to drink more beer and whiskey. Ben could hold his liquor just fine, but after consuming 2 glasses of whiskey sours and 5 pints of beer on an empty stomach, his world began spinning at an alarmingly, nauseating rate.

Ben woke up in his apartment, still wearing his crumpled-up suit and stinking of smoke and vomit. His mouth felt fuzzy, as if he'd stuffed pungent cotton balls into it before crashing on his bed. A swarm of bees buzzed in his head, stinging his skull and swelling his brain. He'd like nothing more than to call in sick and deal with the hangover in quiet solitude. However, the look on Mr. Hisashi's face when Ben almost declined the drink invitation still haunted him. He didn't want to imagine the crushing feeling of disappointment from his boss.

Groaning, he stumbled into the tiny bathroom and took off his dirty clothes. He winced when he came in contact with his skin. Bleary-eyed, Ben inspected his body in front of the mirror. It was covered in small bruises where puncture wounds rested in the middle. He frowned. Had he been attacked by mosquitoes on his way home last night? He didn't know they were that vicious in Japan, to be able to pierce the skin through layers of clothes. As he showered, he made a mental note to grab a repellent from the pharmacy on his way home. Despite his stomach disagreeing of any sustenance, Ben popped three painkillers into his mouth and finished off a *Pocari Sweat* before heading off to work.

Ben was not surprised to see everyone in his department already hard at work, their fingers furiously tapping on the keyboard. What did surprise him, though, was that almost everyone showed no signs of a hangover or exhaustion. The older coworkers' skin wasn't waxy and dark circles didn't dominate their eyes like Ben's. Lethargy didn't seem to have them at a choke-hold. All except Ogawa, that is. The young graduate was on the brink of collapse as he squinted at the computer, trying to make sense of the numbers.

"Hey, are you okay?" Ben asked as he took a seat at his desk.

Ogawa's neck creaked like a rusty door when he turned to Ben. His eyes were glazed and he was much paler than usual. Small circular bruises dotted his neck and his forearms. They looked the same as the ones Ben sported. Guess the mosquitoes had their own buffet last night.

"You know, if you're feeling sick, it's okay to go home," Ben said, hoping that Ogawa would take the bait so he'd have the same excuse to not work.

Fear eclipsed Ogawa's eyes. He glanced skittishly at Mr. Hisashi and the others who were still working, not breaking a sweat at the vicious typing. Ogawa quietly shook his head. "I'm fine. I just need some water."

Ben watched him shuffle to the water cooler in the corner. If he himself wasn't so used to binge drinking on the weekends like he'd done back in his college years, would he look like Ogawa, a walking corpse?

"Good morning, Ben," Mr. Hisashi boomed and slapped Ben on the arm. His supervisor looked as energetic as ever. In fact, his skin seemed to shine with radiance. Maybe it was the harsh lighting in the ceiling, but Ben thought he had more hair on his head. "How are you feeling?"

The spot where Mr. Hisashi had slapped him stung, as if a vein had burst beneath the skin. Ben discreetly rubbed it while smiling at his supervisor. "Good, Mr. Hisashi. A bit tired, but still eager to work."

Mr. Hisashi's own smile was wide and toothy—an uncommon thing for a Japanese *salaryman* to do. "That's great, because the financial department at Iroha.co, our daughter company, just emailed us and requested we go over *their* tax forms."

Ben blanched. "Does that mean—?"

Mr. Hisashi nodded gravely, though his unnerving smile was still etched upon his face. "We're going to have to work overtime tonight as well. But don't worry, we'll go out for drinks afterwards."

Ben only nodded and sunk into his chair. Could he survive two nights of binge drinking in a row?

"That isn't a problem with you, is it, Ben?" Mr. Hisashi's face got eerily closer to Ben's personal space, his eyes almost bulging quizzically.

Ben *wanted* to say it was a problem, that he was still battling his hangover and getting shit-faced again was not going to help with the recovery. *Don't be the nail that sticks out.* He swallowed his discomfort and waved his hand in dismissal. "Not at all. Looking forward to it."

It was like experiencing groundhog day; the same day being repeated with numbers added or subtracted on the computer till Ben's fingers cramped. Then pretending to be as excited as Mr. Hisashi and the other coworkers to go downtown for another long night of drinks and blackout. Disassociating felt easier this time around as Ben focused on getting drunker faster, chugging beer after beer until his stomach acid stank of hops.

The next morning was the same agony as the last one; foggy and smelling of vomit and regrets. Somehow, he did vaguely remember being pinched a lot before he got home. The puncture wounds from the mosquitoes either hadn't healed or a fresh army had snacked on his blood. Ben felt physically weak, like he was going through a nasty flu. His body ached and he had no strength in his limbs. Anemia clutched his veins. Maybe the constant drinking and no sleep resulted in catching something akin to a flu?

Whatever it was, Ben had now a good enough excuse to not show up for work. He didn't want to infect anyone else if he was indeed sick. He justified it further by thinking his work could get worse if he wasn't at his best.

The disappointment in Mr. Hisashi's voice when Ben called in sick slithered into Ben's ear and soured his already churning stomach. "Oh, that's too bad. We still have some work that needs to be done by the end of the day, but hopefully we can manage without you."

Guilt rippling through him, Ben almost told him he'd show up. His foot hovered above the floor from his bed. As he straightened, a wave of nausea struck him. One more movement and his carpet would be spattered with vomit. He apologized to Mr. Hisashi once again and hung up. The guilty feeling coiled his gut. Was he being a bad employee now? Would the others understand his plight? Ben groaned and threw the duvet over his head. Rest was more important than some stupid guilt trip.

Ben ended up sleeping for almost two days.

When he woke up, he felt good enough to walk about. Despite being unconscious for that long, he had remembered to keep the windows closed so the mosquitoes would leave him alone. The small puncture wounds had transformed into slight bruises that could be concealed with Band-aids or flesh-colored lotion. Stomach rumbling, Ben went to check what he had in the fridge. Nothing but a sour stench of an expired *bento* box wafted to his nostrils when he opened it. It made sense since he hadn't had something good to eat for four days.

Ben hesitated. Mr. Hisashi probably thought he was still sick at home. Could he risk going outside for some quick grocery shopping? He scoffed at his uncertainty. It wasn't like he would run into them if they were still at the company, crunching numbers.

He shook off his anxiety, got dressed and headed out. He had a sudden craving for burritos, but he knew the only shop that sold

Mexican ingredients was at Kaldi, which was located downtown. Ben embraced the chilly evening air. It soothed the bruised irritations on his neck and arms. He had to remember to get some balm for it on the way home. As he got closer to downtown, his thoughts drifted to Ogawa. He had been looking rather sickly the other day as well. Was he also absent from work, or did his Japanese diligence overpower him in the end?

A familiar, raucous laughter reached Ben's ears that sent shivers down his spine. He knew exactly who had that laugh since it had been echoing in his mind the last couple nights. It was the last person he wanted to see. Ducking inside a nearby convenience store, Ben had a discreet way of looking outside. Sure enough, Mr. Hisashi and his band of subordinates walked past the store, with Ogawa trailing behind them.

Ben's stomach plummeted at the sight of his young coworker; His face was deathly pale and his cheeks were sunken to the point his cheekbones could cut glass. The light seemed to be fading from his exhausted eyes. While his face was as white as a sheet, the rest of his bony body sported purple, brown and blue bruises where large, circular indents marred his skin in the middle. The poor man looked on the verge of death.

Ben gritted his teeth, fingers balling up into fists. Those bastards were working him to the extremes and they didn't seem to care. Were they going to the same *nomihodai* restaurant? Ben lingered for a while in the store, not wanting to seem like a stalker. Usually he didn't like meddling into affairs that wasn't his business, but this involved a newcomer like him. Whether they had anything in common or not, he *had* to see if Ogawa was going to be all right in his, what, third or fourth *nomikai?*

It had to be considered some kind of work abuse. What was the term the Japanese had made for stress-related deaths? *Karoshi?* The constant binge-drinking and then working like a racehorse the next day without rest would be a likely cause. Ben had to make sure Ogawa wouldn't fall victim to it.

Ben peered up at the old, neon sign that blinked precariously above the dingy building. He hadn't given it much thought the first time he went there as he'd blindly followed his supervisor, but why would Mr. Hisashi and his crew choose to go to that restaurant when there were a bunch of various establishments that looked a lot cleaner surrounding the area? Ben steeled himself and marched up the open cement stairs, following the same steps he'd taken twice already.

The restaurant was located in the middle of the building. Ben had to double-check if he had gone the wrong way, though. The door to the eatery was hardly marked. There was a small sign taped by the wall with an arrow pointing to the door. A stale odor of fried oil and beer lingered by the entrance.

Ben frowned. Why go through all the trouble of making an eatery so hidden? Wouldn't that defeat the purpose of luring customers in, or was it some kind of speakeasy? It was funny how he never asked Mr. Hisashi about it, or maybe he did but couldn't remember after all the drinking?

Ben took a deep breath, opened the door and stepped inside.

Clouds of smoke obscured the interior of the restaurant. Waving the toxic fumes away and coughing, Ben made his way further inside. Low, traditional Japanese music played in the background, but raucous, over-zealous laughter from other patrons overpowered it. Ben gazed around to see if he spotted the middle-aged supervisor and his subordinates. It was like finding an honest man in Congress. Every single customer was either a middle-aged or elderly office worker. He managed to locate a cheery-looking waitress who bowed deeply while balancing a tray full of liquor on her hand.

"Did a group from Sankyo arrive a few minutes ago?" he asked in bad Japanese.

The waitress's smile faltered. "Why do you ask?" she asked in perfect English as her eyes flitted behind Ben.

Ben balked. There was no turning back now. "I was invited to a *nomikai*, but got held up at the doctor's. Mr. Hisashi from Sankyo told me to come here, but he forgot to tell me which room he'd booked."

Realization dawned on the waitress and a big smile spread across her painted lips. "*Of course* you're here for the *nomikai*. How silly of me to think otherwise. Mr. Hisashi is in room four."

She turned around and made her way toward the narrow hallway that contained the private rooms reserved for bigger groups. Ben grabbed her arm and gently pulled her back. She looked at him curiously.

"There's no need to inform him of my arrival. I want it to be a surprise," he said with a sly wink.

The waitress's eyes narrowed slightly, as if she was mad that he was barring her from doing her job, but she erased it with a polite smile. "Of course. Have it your way," she said and scurried off to the bar, where the bartender, a tall, lean man, stared at Ben with such intensity it made his skin crawl.

In fact, the whole place gave him the creeps. He'd better hurry up, grab Ogawa, and get the hell out of there. Then he'd hand in his resignation the first thing in the morning. No way he'd waste his life in this kind of work environment.

He hurried across the hallway, glad the loud noises coming from each room deafened his stomping footsteps.

The door to room four stood before him. For the third time this evening, Ben hesitated. He had no idea how he would do this. Barge in like some white knight and grab the young graduate without a word to his supervisor? As far-fetched and cringy as it was, it seemed like the best way of doing it, but Ben wasn't sure if he could *actually* do it. Would it be better to fake a family emergency? Would they buy it?

Only one way to find out.

Ben had his hand on the doorknob, ready to turn it and storm inside when he heard something from inside the room. It wasn't the usual, raucous laughter that he remembered from the previous events. Furrowing his brow, Ben leaned in and pressed his ear against the wood. Eerie stillness held the room, except for some low whimpers and—was that slurping?

There was no keyhole on the door so he couldn't peek through. Morbid curiosity overwhelmed him. Ben opened the door just a crack and peeped.

His scream lodged in his throat.

Ogawa lay on the long table, his shirt ripped open and dangling from his sides, his bare chest on full display.

Circling him were Mr. Hisashi and the other middle-aged subordinates, their backs hunched over and rocking back and forth. Viscous saliva drooled down on the floor from their gaping mouths. Six, thin, long needle-like appendages stretched out of all of their mouths and pierced deep into Ogawa's flesh. They groaned and slurped in pleasure as crimson liquid pumped from the man's puncture wounds and traveled to their mouth-parts.

Ogawa's sunken cheeks grew more prominent, his skin brittle and paler each time his superiors sucked his blood. His breath rattled, as if the men were absorbing the air from his lungs as well. He gave a final convulsive jerk and went limp, the light finally leaving his eyes.

"Oh, Mr. Hisashi, I'm afraid we've drained him already," Ikeda, one of Mr. Hisashi's devoted subordinates, said while the needles retracted back into his mouth with a hideous gurgle.

Mr. Hisashi prodded Ogawa's body with his knee and grunted. "That's a shame. I thought we could use him for a few more days. I guess he wasn't cut out for this line of work." He barked a cruel laugh. "No youth can handle the responsibilities that we carry on our shoulders."

"Shall I notify Corporate about his death? Let them know it was stress-related?"

Mr. Hisashi's smile grew wide as a toad who had swallowed a juicy fly. "Of course. We'll have to mention that they'll need to advertise for the position again."

Ikeda nodded and whipped up a notepad from his suitcase. He began writing in the same furious, mechanical way he'd done back at the office.

Ben's eyes widened further, feet rooted to the floor. The skin on Mr. Hisashi, Ikeda, and the others stretched and smoothed. Any wrinkles, crow's feet and tiredness vanished, as if they'd dipped their faces into the Fountain of Youth. Vertebrae cracked as their back straightened. Mr. Hisashi's paunchy stomach thinned little by little, like someone had cut a slice of it with a knife. He patted it affectionately.

"Only a few more *nomikais* and I'll be back to my youthful days," he said with a chuckle.

"We've got Ben left," Ikeda pointed out while he checked out the voluminous hair that had grown over his bald patch.

Mr. Hisashi gave an annoyed grunt. "If he bothers to come back to work, that is."

"Do you think he suspects something?"

Mr. Hisashi scoffed. "No, I think he's a lazy American. That's all."

That was Ben's cue to get the hell out of there. He didn't know where to go from here, though. Back to his cramped apartment, where the company knew where he lived? Should he leave the country? It was the safest option for him, if he wanted to stay alive. He straightened and turned around.

The waitress and the bartender stood in front of him, wearing those two-faced polite smiles.

"Going somewhere?" the waitress asked sweetly. A tray full of alcoholic beverages she held in her other hand blocked the right side.

Ben stood frozen. He could probably push the waitress aside, but the bartender was more muscular up close. He blocked Ben's left side of exit.

Cold beads of sweat pearled on his temple. "J-Just g-going to the bathroom," he stammered and inched a little to the side.

The bartender smirked, leaned over and opened the door to the private room. "The honored guest has arrived, gentlemen. I hope you enjoy a foreign taste for the rest of the evening."

The waitress strolled inside with the tray while the bartender pushed Ben over the threshold. The fear of death had rendered him immobile and sobbing.

Mr. Hisashi's smile was big enough to devour him.

"*Kanpai!*"

THE HAG'S GIFT

I'm certain my next-door neighbor has been stealing my milk.

We both live on the ground floor and she gets up at the crack of dawn before the milkman arrives. There are always fresh tobacco spits on the pavement when I go out. I want to confront her about it, but she's … weird.

One of the upstairs neighbors informed me once that she was from Iceland. Are all Icelanders this creepy? Her white hair is unkempt and frayed, like a spider's web. Instead of wrinkles and liver spots, her skin is pale, frail, and paper-thin. Might be the reason she doesn't smile at all. Her eyes are the worst; one is big and icy blue while the other is lazy with white fog obscuring it.

The way she looks at me and my newborn baby with those eyes from the window, especially when I'm out on my daily walks, is unnerving. Is she after my baby? I get shivers just thinking about it.

But I've had it. I won't have her use *my* things for whatever witchy schemes she's brewing.

It's been a week since I stopped having my milk delivered. My creepy neighbor hasn't made a fuss. In fact, she hasn't been out of her apartment all week. I know since I've been home-bound on maternity leave since I've had my baby.

She hasn't stopped watching me through the window. The creep factor has turned up another notch. Instead of standing there and staring like usual, she's nursing something wrapped in ratty, gray wool. I don't know what it is—I don't dare come any closer to that hag—but it's like she's mocking me. Every time I glance in her direction at the beginning and end of my walks, she juts her chin and places the thing between her sagging breasts, mimicking the way I hold the baby in my arms.

My scalp prickles and I hurry out of sight, shielding my child. Damn hag. Not only has she stolen my milk, but she's trying to rob me of crucial bonding time with my baby.

I dream that mice gather around me. One by one, they nibble at my flesh. The ones chewing on my toes tickle. I twitch when they come closer. The hairs on the back of my neck stand on end when their fur touches me.

Then a scraggly one climbs up my chest and sniffs my left nipple. I stiffen in the dream, my muscles tense. It's as if it knows that area is sensitive. I wince when its tiny teeth clamp onto it. Should I be feeling pain in my dream? I should wake up; this unnerving dream is turning into a nightmare.

My brows furrow as I struggle to open my eyes. Something's wrong. The air is cold. Did I leave the window open? Is my baby all right? I raise my arm. It stays put at my side. I frown and try again. It's like dead weight. My chest heaves from dread. Why can't I move? My breath quickens and I focus all my energy to open my eyes. They flutter. I instantly turn to the side to check on the crib.

My chin trembles. My throat constricts and traps my voice. Rushed thrashing in my ears.

A grotesque, worm-like creature, wrapped in dirty, old wool curls up on my belly and sucks on my teat. Its suction-cupped mouth bulges with each gulp and its bony tip stings my navel.

Bile builds up in my throat. I manage only a twitch of a leg or an arm. I can't swat it away. I let out a terrified whimper.

Its horribly pink, shriveled head looks up at me. Chills surge through me. Its eyes are mismatched—one big and blue, the other slightly foggy. Its mouth splits into a wide smile, showing me rows of tiny, sharp teeth. Its voice is high-pitched, like a rat's squeak. "If Mamma can't get her milk normally, I will get it for her."

My stomach sinks. *She* sent that vile creature. She couldn't leave me alone. My strength slips away as it resumes sucking on my raw nipple.

My heartbeat drums slower. Cold seeps into my skin and freezes the tissue. My eyelids grow heavier.

It is sucking me dry.

That damn hag …

The Yule Lads Are Coming

oud bleating from outside his house in the west of Iceland woke Hallgrímur Ásgrímsson up from his deep slumber.

He groaned and stumbled out of bed while rubbing the crust of sleep off his eyes. His sheep were usually quiet at night, so there was only one reason they'd make a sound like that; either a mink or a fox had sneaked into their den to nibble on a defenseless lamb.

"Won't be long. I'm taking the rifle just in case," he said.

No one replied. His bed had only occupied him, yet he always assumed his late wife would respond. Always thought they'd be together forever.

Hallgrímur shook his head, pushing the grief that threatened to flood his heart to the back of his mind. He quickly put on clothes and shuffled through the hallway, careful not to wake up his son, Hákon, in the next room. While putting on his lopapeysa—an Icelandic, handknitted, woolen sweater—Hallgrímur opened the locked storage closet and pulled out the rifle. He rarely used it, only during hunting seasons, but kept a couple of rounds nearby for situations such as these.

He really didn't want to deal with minks or foxes right now. There were only thirteen days till Christmas, and he already had enough on his plate, what with sending smoked lamb to the local stores and taking care of his son. People had begun supporting local farms instead of the megafarms the past few years and Hallgrímur had been busy preparing for this year's demand.

He loaded the rifle and opened the front door, braving himself for the cold and the snow that usually piled on in December.

He peered down at the white fluff beneath his feet, expecting to see little animal paw prints. He frowned. Two circular dents dotted the snow, starting from outside Hákon's window and leading to the sheep's den.

"What the fuck …" he muttered, scratching his chin. What kind of animal had that paw print? He leaned down to get a closer look, thinking that one of the sheep must have escaped their humble abode and had wandered off near the house. He banished the thought. Sheep had hooves and those prints were completely circular, like someone had used a baton or something.

A sheep let out a sharp, painful cry.

Hallgrímur's head whipped up. Something was still bothering his livestock. He gripped his rifle and trudged through the snow, following the trail.

The den smelled of dirty wool and dank hay. The place was dark, yet he spotted fluffy animals shambling together for warmth. Hallgrímur couldn't afford a ceiling light like some farmers, but he knew the sheep wouldn't know the difference. After all, they were stupid.

Something crunched in the gravel. Hard, almost hollow sound. Not at all like hooves stomping the ground.

"Who's there?" Hallgrímur called as he fished out his cell phone.

A sheep whined a cry for help. The other ones herded away into the far most corner of the den, as if avoiding being attacked by whatever was inside. Hallgrímur squinted into the darkness. Something hunched over the animal. Suckling sounds—reminding Hallgrímur of the time Hákon had been on the bottle as an infant—echoed in the tiny chamber.

The hair at the back of Hallgrímur's neck stood on end. He pocketed the butt of the rifle into his shoulder. He turned on his phone's flashlight, spotlighting the white, puffy quadrupeds.

He froze, almost dropping his phone.

A bearded man, on his knees, bent his torso at an angle Hallgrímur thought wasn't humanly possible. He wore old, woolen clothes, older than Hallgrímur's lopapeysa. They reminded him of the clothes he had seen on display at the National Museum of Iceland, especially the long, red cap that dangled precariously on top of the man's head. His mouth suckled on the sheep's teat. That wasn't the creepiest thing. He didn't have any legs.

Instead of legs of bones and flesh, wooden pegs tapped against the hardened ground, in beat to the ferocious sucking.

"What the fuck?" Hallgrímur spluttered, his stomach churning at the sight. "Get away from my sheep, you sicko!"

The old man looked him straight in the eyes, *grinned* and ignored him, holding even tighter to the sheep's wool. His knuckles turned stark white, tugging the teat harder. The poor animal squirmed in pain.

Hallgrímur flushed, taken aback by the man's behavior. He'd thought it was just a vagrant, seeking shelter from the cold, but he hadn't heard of vagrants stealing sheep's milk right from their teats. He raised his gun and cocked it. "I'm warning you."

At the sound of the gun being ready to fire, the man let go of the poor creature. It scampered away, whining bloody murder. The man still sat on his knees; arms raised up in surrender.

"I apologize, good sir. It has been a long walk to all these houses here and I'm afraid I got too thirsty for my liking. Your sheep are fine animals. Their milk will keep me going for the rest of the trip." The man's face split into a toothy grin. Frothy milk covered the man's yellowish teeth and coated his beard.

"What's your name?" Hallgrímur demanded, still not lowering the gun.

The man chuckled. "Oh, you know who I am. I used to come by your window every year when you were a child. Gave you treats if you were nice, or potatoes if you were naughty."

So, he was a peeping tom as well as a thief? "Still going to need that name."

The man's mirth continued. "I don't have time for this. I've got other houses to see. Other children to watch."

He stood, his peg legs banging on the frozen ground. Hallgrímur flinched and pulled the trigger. The shot boomed in the shed and the rifle's recoil hit Hallgrímur hard on the shoulder. Ears ringing, he rubbed his sore spot and looked around for the bearded intruder.

He was on the ground. His belly faced the ceiling. Blood oozed from a huge, pulpy wound in the middle of his chest. Was a wound supposed to look like strawberry jam? Crimson bubbled from his gasping mouth. Copper tang and sour milk mixed with the musty air.

"Oh, shit. Oh, shit, shit, shit!" Hallgrímur dropped the gun and scurried over to the man he shot.

The bearded man's eyes bulged as his trembling hands tried to cover the wound. The flesh around it had ripped to ribbons, sticking to the soaked woolen sweater. Hallgrímur kneeled next to him, though he was unsure what he was supposed to do. If he performed CPR, wouldn't all the blood just spurt upwards from the wound? Should he call an ambulance? It'd be too late since his farm was an hour away from the nearest town.

He gasped when the man's hand clutched his arm and using his last ounce of strength, pulled Hallgrímur closer to him.

"Naughty …" The man whispered; a sinister smile etched on his bloody face as his last breath dragged through a painful rattle.

Hallgrímur's heart pounded against his ribs. He had killed a man. And there were only thirteen days till Christmas.

This year couldn't get any worse.

He pried the dead man's hand off his arm and stood up, gazing at the body. He decided then and there. He was *not* going to jail over this. No one had heard the gun being shot. No one had heard anything and if by some twisted sense of irony Hulda, his next-door neighbor heard it, he'd tell her it'd just been a fox.

He dragged the body by the hands—he feared the pegs would pop off if he pulled on them—and brought it to the compost area near the barn. The soil that wasn't completely frozen, due to the warm water running underneath, was the perfect spot to bury the body. He grabbed a shovel and dug a hole big enough for the old man. Sweat slicked his back and his joints creaked and ached, but he didn't pause for a second. He wanted to get this done before morning.

A distant screech whistled through the air. Frowning, Hallgrímur stopped and listened. It sounded like sorrowful wailing but coming from a great distance away. He turned to the mountains that faced his farm. Was someone trapped there in the middle of the night? Hallgrímur waited for the sound to come again, but it never came. He shrugged and with the last ounce of his strength, rolled the body into the hole.

Once buried, Hallgrímur spread fresh hay on the den's floor to disguise the blood and splashed a bucket of water on the wall. He then locked the gun inside the closet.

It was done. Only he knew what had happened. Only he had to live with it. And he was going to take it to his grave.

The next day went without a hitch. Hallgrímur kept himself busy with preparing the meat in the smoking chamber. A knock on the door and Hulda walked in. She was too young to be widowed like him, but he appreciated the connection they had with it. She had been supportive, helping with the meat and spending time with Hákon. He was unsure if he liked it or not. But every time she showed up, he couldn't ignore the swooping sensation in his belly.

"I heard something like a shot last night," she said.

Hallgrímur blushed. "Oh, yeah, a damn fox tried to take one of the lambs. I had to shoot it."

She winced, muttering "poor thing," as she heaved another leg of lamb onto a free hook that lined the walls. Hallgrímur didn't want to admit it to himself, but he loved how she cared about the animals. Hallgrímur's guilt only lingered for a moment, then he remembered he had better things to do.

Two days after the incident, Hulda unexpectedly came over at breakfast. She held up a casserole dish full of lasagna and a bright smile.

"I made too much lasagna last night and I figured you might want some."

Hallgrímur's mouth twitched. "You shouldn't have."

"Nonsense. I know you don't eat as much during this time of the month, and I don't want you collapsing from hunger." Hulda went straight for the fridge and put the dish inside. She then grabbed a cup of coffee, sat down next to him, and patted his arm.

Warmth travelled from Hallgrímur's chest to his fingers. "Thank you. I know Hákon will be pleased."

As if on cue, Hákon came into the kitchen, frowning and holding something in his hand. Hallgrímur jumped out of the chair, away from Hulda's nice smelling hair.

"What's the matter, buddy? Why the long face?" Hallgrímur asked, bemused.

"Gully Gawk didn't leave me anything in my shoe. Just this note."

Hallgrímur's brows furrowed. It was an old tradition in Iceland that the Yule Lads, benign half-trolls, came down from the mountains thirteen nights before Christmas and left either treats or potatoes in children's shoe that they left on their windowsill. It all depended on if they had behaved well or were little demanding monsters. It was just folklore, of course, but parents still use it as an incentive to make their children behave through all the stress leading up to Christmas.

"Let me see that note."

Hákon handed his father the piece of wrinkled, old paper, and took a seat with his arms crossed.

Hallgrímur smoothed out the paper. The handwriting was crude, with angry blotches of ink spilled to the side, as if the writer's hand had been trembling with rage. His brows burrowed deeper near the center of his forehead as he read the single sentence: *We know what you did.*

"Is someone bullying you at school, Hákon?" he asked.

Hákon shook his head, his chin nestled in his chest.

Hallgrímur glanced at Hulda, who gave an uncertain shrug. She didn't know him well enough, of course.

"Don't worry, honey. I'm sure Gully Gawk had been so busy that he forgot your house. Tell you what, I'll personally write him a note, telling him how well behaved you were and Stubby will probably give something nice." Hulda said, ruffling Hákon's hair affectionately.

Hallgrímur's heart swelled. She didn't need to, but he saw the determination in her eyes. He suddenly wished that he had dressed in better clothes. Hulda offered to take him to school, but Hallgrímur decided to do it himself so that he could have a word with Hákon's teacher.

The school reported nothing, but over the next couple of days, something odd happened at the Ásgrímsstaðir farm.

All of the pans disappeared from the kitchen yet there was no evidence of a break in.

Their bowls reeked of urine for which Hallgrímur blamed the dog, but Hulda, chuckling in one of her visits, doubted the dog could jump atop the cabinets, open them with his paws and pee into all the bowls and then stack them neatly in their proper place. It was weird but nothing that the dishwasher couldn't clean. It turned into an evening of laughs and wine.

Hallgrímur began anticipating Hulda's visits and tried cleaning the house in the evenings to make a better impression. He danced on his toes, imagining Hulda's surprised expression as he went to sleep after a good cleanup.

Hulda's screams woke Hallgrímur up the next morning. Thinking she had injured herself, he rushed into the kitchen. A stink so repellant punched him in the nostrils.

He recoiled. "What the fuck is that stench?" he asked as he covered his nose and mouth with his hand.

Eyes watering from the stink, Hulda, wrapped in a nice dress, pointed at all the pots strewn around the kitchen floor. Something yellowish brown stewed in each of them. Some semi-solid chunks floated in them.

"I-Is that shit?"

Hulda nodded. "Don't you dare blame it on the dog, Hallgrímur. This is getting more than weird. I think someone is harassing you. You need to report it to the police."

Hallgrímur's cheeks reddened in embarrassment. No way he could impress her now. He led Hulda out of the putrid stench and into the living room. "I don't have proof. These things seem to always happen when Hákon and I are asleep, even the dog, and even if someone *had* broken in, the dog would have known." He glanced at the kitchen door, nose wrinkling as the foul odor invaded all the rooms, then down at his neighbor. "Now, be straight with me, *you* haven't been having any stomach problems recently? Like irritable bowel syndrome or something?"

Hulda's nostrils flared. She yanked her hand back and stomped towards the front door. "For even *suggesting* that *I'm* behind this, you'll be cleaning that shit up."

Hallgrímur cursed loudly as he scratched his scalp furiously. If it was not her and it certainly wasn't him, who could have done it? He stared at Hákon's bedroom door. Could his son be doing it? For some kind of desperate attention? For revenge because he still hadn't received a single treat from the supposed Yule Lads?

Wait a minute …

He flashed through the last couple of days in his mind. Pans disappearing. Stubby had been known for doing that. The bowls could be traced to Bowl-Licker, though his method had changed drastically. And instead of stealing leftovers from the pots, Pot-Scraper had *left* them shitty leftovers.

Hallgrímur's stomach churned when he realized that he had forgotten about Spoon-Licker and how all their spoons had probably been licked by him.

That left seven Yule Lads. One more week of annoying pranks.

The pranks got worse.

Hallgrímur and his son couldn't get a wink of sleep because all the doors of the house kept slamming by themselves. Hulda hadn't visited those mornings and Hallgrímur missed seeing her heart-shaped face. Swallowing his pride, he went over to her house and apologized. With pursed lips, Hulda let him in and allowed him to tell her about his sleepless nights. She was convinced the home was haunted and wanted to call a priest to purify it. Hallgrímur let her. It was better than telling her his own suspicions of half-trolls from old legends actually existing. And that he had killed one of their brothers. He didn't want to lose her if she thought that he had gone crazy.

The ninth night was the worst by far. Again, Hallgrímur jumped at Hulda's screams. He ran outside to the sheep den. His curses got lodged in his throat and he had to turn away, but the sight was forever burned in his retina.

A couple of his sheep lay dead on the ground. Their stomachs slit open and their intestines dragged out of their cavities. They had all been twisted in intervals, to resemble disgustingly pink links of sausages. Tiny maggots slithered through open holes.

"Who would do this?" Hulda sobbed as she tried to ward the dog from eating the viscera.

Hallgrímur knew. This was Sausage-Swiper's doing. Who'd known he was that sick in the mind? To go after defenseless animals, just for a prank?

"You have to report this, Hallgrímur. Someone is out there to get you. I don't want you to get hurt over this." Hulda wiped her tears as she turned to him.

Hallgrímur was taken aback at the dark circles underneath her eyes. Her pallid complexion. Was she that worried about him? Did she care so much? He was even more surprised to see the same face reflected in her eyes. They were both exhausted, having to deal with this crap while preparing for Christmas. But they were in this together. It was perhaps morbid that the death of his sheep finally brought them together, but at that moment, Hallgrímur didn't care. He pulled her in a hug, embracing her warmth. She reciprocated, held tight to his back.

He heaved a great sigh, though his eyes burned in a different matter. "Don't worry. I'll take care of it."

On December 23rd, Hallgrímur had the chair lined up towards the front door. He sat down with his rifle on his lap. Hulda slept in his bedroom, after she insisted she stay over to make sure that both him and Hákon would be all right. A smile tugged at Hallgrímur's lips. At least there'd be one thing to look forward to on Christmas Eve. The last three days hadn't been as bad as the day the sheep were killed.

They had only noticed a face print on all of their windows, as if someone had been glued to it the entire night (Window-Peeper for sure) and all of Hulda's homemade leaf bread that she had given them had been swiped and thrown into the compost (Doorway-Sniffer loved leaf bread). The last straw had been the work of Meat-Hook. He had broken into the smoking chamber and destroyed all the meat hanging in there. Now he couldn't sell his meat to the stores.

So, he was going to be ready to meet the last one, Candle-Stealer. They had already ruined everything. Hallgrímur didn't care anymore if he killed another one of those bastards. He'd be ridding Iceland of those pests and then parents wouldn't be forced to give kids thirteen small gifts before getting even more on Christmas.

It was well after midnight and Hallgrímur heard nothing. He glanced at the window, seeing white snow flutter down ceremoniously hailing Christmas Eve. They'd be blessed with both white Christmas *and* red, if the damn Yule Lad showed up.

He sipped his energy drink, grimacing at the foul, artificial flavor, but he figured it'd be more effective than coffee.

Yet, he felt sluggish, his muscles going limp and heavy. He stifled a yawn with his fist and resisted the urge to slap his own cheeks. He just needed to stand up and walk around. His feet were rooted to the spot. He wanted to knead his thighs, but his arms were nestled comfortably on his lap and moving them seemed like a crime. His eyelids grew heavier and heavier, fluttering at the pace of his slow beating heart.

Hallgrímur jerked awake at the sound of whimpers. Did the dog have to go out?

"Settle down," he groaned and made to stand up.

He couldn't. The whimpers increased in volume, though he had no idea where they were coming from. He glanced down. Ice crusted around his heart. His wrists were tied to his dining room chair. Bound with old, smelly rope.

"What the hell?" he muttered and tried to wiggle his arms. They were securely fastened. He hitched in a breath at the rope burn.

"Look who's finally awake, brothers." A gravely voice said in the darkness of the living room.

Hallgrímur peered into the room, his heart doing jumping jacks as shapes moved towards the light of the foyer. Twelve men approached him. All bearded, wearing clothes suited for the 19th century. They stank of old sweat and anger. Two of them dragged chairs behind them; Hulda and Hákon, gagged and bound, occupied them.

"Oh my god," Hallgrímur whispered, air draining of his lungs.

Tears streaked their frightened faces as they looked from Hallgrímur and the twelve invaders. Why had Hallgrímur let Hulda stay? He hated himself for getting them both mixed up in this ordeal.

The one who seemed to have the kindest temperament kneeled in front of Hallgrímur. He had old-timey spectacles, a round nose and wrinkles across his mouth and eyes. Laugh-lines his mother would always call it. But that man wasn't smiling or laughing.

"Hello, Hallgrímur. I'm sure you know who we are."

Hallgrímur spotted candles sticking out of his pocket. "I thought you'd never show up, Candle-Stealer."

Candle-Stealer chuckled. "Of course, I would. But we always come when we get you all to fall asleep. Can't steal those candles if someone is awake."

Hallgrímur glared at the other Yule Lads who either sat or stood around them, not looking jolly, but threatening. A whiff of something sour and tangy wafted from the fattest Yule Lad, who had his hand deep in a big, wooden barrel. Thinking nobody would see, he scooped up a handful of skyr into his mouth.

"You're not here for the candles, though, are you?"

Candle-Stealer shook his head. "No. You killed our brother, Sheep-Cote Clod, simply because he was thirst—"

"He broke into my sheep den and harassed my sheep!" Hallgrímur interrupted him, outraged. "Only a sick psychopath does that."

Candle-Stealer slapped him hard across the cheek. Hallgrímur's ears rang and he let out a stream of curses while the stinging pain in his cheek subsided.

"Don't you dare speak that way about my brother. He was a good man, who loved children. You just couldn't see past your prejudice."

The rest of the Yule Lads murmured in agreement. One with calloused hands and splinters sticking out of them stood up abruptly. "Let me slap him too, brother," he snarled.

Candle-Stealer held up a hand. "No, Door-Slammer. It's time we end this." He rose up, his frame towering over Hallgrímur.

Dread seeped into Hallgrímur's veins, shrinking them within his system. The tips of his toes felt numb, as if he were soaking them in a partly frozen lake. Hallgrímur's eyes darted from the woman he loved and his son to the grinning faces of the Yule Lads. "What do you intend to do?" His dry mouth let out the question before he could stop himself.

The smallest of the bunch trotted to Candle-Stealer, holding two glass candle jars, marked with the letter 'H'. Hulda's eyes widened and she writhed against the rope, her whimpers muffled. Hallgrímur realized that she had planned on giving him and Hákon those candles. The light emitting from them cast an unpleasant shadow across the Yule Lad's smiling face. Hallgrímur saw nothing but bloodlust.

"An eye for an eye, Hallgrímur. It's only fair." Candle-Stealer said as he accepted the candles, examining the warm, wax-like liquid swirling in the jars. He looked up and gave his brothers a curt nod.

One Yule Lad, who smelled strongly of smoked lamb, grabbed Hallgrímur's chair and tilted him backwards. Two others came up on either side of him and peeled back his eyelids with grimy fingers. Hallgrímur cursed and spat, writhing in his chair, and tried with all his might to replace his ever-increasing fear with rage.

"No, please, stop! I'm sorry, I didn't mean to kill your brother, I swear."

"Too little, too late, Hallgrímur. If you had repented in the first place, things probably would have been different." Candle-Stealer said, the jars of flaming liquid hovering mere inches from Hallgrímur's eyes. The smell of cinnamon and cloves tickled his nose. It should have brought forth a comforting feeling in his chest—a feeling of warmth. Not the ice-cold sweat that slicked his back. It shouldn't be constricting his throat.

"Please don—"

His words transformed into screams of agony as Candle-Stealer poured wax into his open eyes. Instinct hit his brain and demanded him to shut them close, but the Yule Lads held a firm grip. His corneas blistered, a white-hot sear trickling into his skull like fire ants.

Hallgrímur screamed until his throat felt raw. His stomach rolled, bile rising from inside. Something luke-warm and sour thrust into his mouth by a rough hand. He gagged but heard sinister chortles through the thrashing in his ears. Another thick glob was forced into his mouth, and he realized that they were force-feeding him skyr, the Icelandic yoghurt. To stop him from screaming. At one point it stopped and all he heard was the smacking of fat lips.

"Stop eating the skyr yourself, Skyr-Gobbler, and shovel more into him." Candle-Stealer commanded as he peeled the dry wax from Hallgrímur's eyes ever so slowly. The blisters popped, warm, white liquid oozed from them. He chuckled at Hallgrímur's jerks and whimpers as the wax plugged each strand of eyelashes. He proceeded to pour a fresh batch of wax into the wounded eyes again. The stench of cinnamon, cloves and burning hair and flesh filled the room.

The air whistled and something cold and solid pierced Hallgrímur's hands and feet. A whiff of smoked lamb as Meat Hook twisted the smoking hooks deeper into his flesh, until bones crunched. Hallgrímur's muscles tensed so much he felt each sinew snap like a guitar string.

"I wonder if this feels the same as killing a sheep and smoke it," Meat Hook grunted in Hallgrímur's ear and the other Yule Lads let out raucous laughs.

After what felt like an eternity, Hallgrímur's screams were mere gurgles, his chin drenched in skyr. His stomach ached horribly from being full of the tangy yoghurt-like substance. Blood streamed from the puncture wounds of his hands and feet. A shivering ache traveled to his abdomen. Tightness clutched his pounding heart. Cold sweat poured from every pore of his body. Despite the overwhelming pain, fatigue enveloped him like a security blanket. And he embraced it fully. Anything to get away from this torture. He felt guilty for leaving Hulda behind. For not telling her how he really felt about her, for thanking her to like a gruff like him. He felt sorry that his son had to witness his death like that, at the hands of someone he thought to be benign and friendly.

I'm sorry, he thought, directing his final words to them. His impaired vision grew darker and darker, until he plunged head-first into oblivion.

"I think he's dead," Stubby squeaked after feeling around Hallgrímur's limp wrists.

"Then our work here is done," Candle-Stealer announced and put the empty candle jars down on the floor. "Release the woman and child. They have done nothing wrong against us."

Sobbing, Hulda immediately stumbled to Hallgrímur's body and cradled his head in her arms.

Hákon stared at the Yule Lads. He had stopped crying, his eyes filled with nothing but hollow disbelief.

"Why?" was all he managed as he watched them getting ready to take off.

Candle-Stealer flashed him a pitiful smile. "Because your father was naughty and needed to be punished. Always remember, little Hákon: Stay on our good side, allow us to do our things in peace and you will be rewarded. If not, well ..." He gestured to the protuberant vein-popping belly, the bloody hooks hanging from the hands and hollowed eyed corpse of his father. "You'll end up like him. Merry Christmas."

And the Yule Lads' forms retreated into the snowy darkness, heading home to the mountains to bring their mother, Grýla, the good news.

THE PERFECT TIME

straighten the folds on my dress and check my makeup in the mirror. The foundation seems to do its job of covering my pores, but the light is too harsh.

"GAIA, warm light, please."

The bathroom's illumination fades until I no longer have to squint my eyes. The rest of the makeup is adequate, but with the limited supplies, it'll have to do. My watch beeps, the cycle app announcing that ovulation has begun. I take a deep breath, put on my best smile and head out.

Evan waits by the door, wearing his best suit. Judging by the constant tapping of his foot, he's just as jittery about this date as I am.

"You look dashing," I say while accepting the artificially created bouquet of flowers he hands me.

"And you're beautiful. Shall we, m'lady?" Evan smiles and leads me where our table is.

It's simple; white tablecloth and aluminum plates and cutlery. A single cube of pressed, dehydrated vegetables and crickets lays on the plates while the glasses are filled with filtered water. I would have preferred wine, but beggars can't be choosers.

"Meal of champions," Evan says lamely as he pushes my chair closer to the table.

There's not even a smell from the cubes, which is good, I guess. I heard from Mom that crickets smell bad. I keep my smile plastered on my face. Evan must have put a lot of thought into preparing for tonight.

"Do you like the view?" He gestures to the window which shows a sunny meadow with grazing cows.

I wrinkle my nose and push the idea of meat being on the menu out of my mind. It hasn't been too long since we rinsed the taste out of our mouths. "Isn't this supposed to be a date *night?*"

Evan chuckles. "Oh, of course. GAIA, could you change the scenery to something dark and romantic?"

GAIA, the motherboard of the home system, obliges and the landscape changes into a starry night over a bonfire. It even adds the sound of the crackling flames to make it seem more authentic.

However, it only brings forth a sense of yearning within me. For a place I'll never get to experience for myself. A thing of the past.

"That's better, right?" Evan asks, his eyes hopeful.

I nod, despite the hollow feeling in my chest.

We eat our dinner in silence, crunching on stale cubes of nutrition. We could chat, but the conversation would be empty words since there's so much we already know about each other. Better to just enjoy the nice presence we share.

"I wish I could bring you dessert or something," Evan says after we finish our meal, looking around the pristine kitchen for a jar of cookies or cake. Of course, none of that exists.

I wave my hand dismissively. "It's fine, the cube should be enough to sustain us for the night."

"But I wish I could give you something sweet. I heard such good things about chocolate," Evan sighs.

Mom used to say it was divine, I think to myself, but instead I say out loud: "You're sweet enough for me."

Evan blushes. Despite myself, my heart flutters at his innocence.

A bell chimes in the distance, signaling that the lights will be extinguished in an hour to save power.

My pulse races. We have an hour left of our date.

"Well, I guess this is it." There's a tone of finality in Evan´s voice as he rises and extends his hand.

Swallowing, I take it and let him lead me to our quarters.

Two doors stand next to each other in the empty hallway. The smell of spoiled meat still lingers in the stagnant air. There used to be more people here underground, but they succumbed to whatever is ailing the earth above. Evan and I are the only ones left.

We stand in front of the doors, as if unsure what to do next.

Though we both know.

"It's time," Evan says and gives me a hollow kiss on the cheek.

I blink through watery eyes and squeeze his hand.

"I'll be gentle," he says as he opens the door to the left. The door on the right belongs to his room. The left is mine.

A mirthless chuckle escapes my lips. I've known Evan since he was a baby. We've been together through thick and thin, even when the world fell apart above and we were forced to live below. Even when we watched Mom and Dad cough their lungs out in short, rattling fits. Even when supplies ran low and the meat of our dead loved ones was a better option than starving to death.

He's always been my kind, little brother, but those times are dead. We've known it for a while but we kept pushing it down. Delaying the inevitable. There's no escaping it now.

A new creation is about to begin.

WHAT PROTECTS OUR HERITAGE: AN ICELANDIC CRYPTID STORY

CHAPTER 1: THE CALL

Droning vibrations drilled into Sigurbjörn's ears, stirring him from a fretful sleep. Feeling like his head was wrapped in cotton, he squinted at the bedside table and groaned. His cellphone whirred continuously, teetering on the edge of the wood. Sigurbjörn didn't want to answer it. He rarely got calls around eleven at night. The only one who would think of calling him at this hour was Ingimundur, the head of Víkverji of the south division of SAR—Iceland's Search and Rescue squad. That would only mean one thing: someone got lost either on one of the glaciers or the mountains nearby. A clueless tourist, no doubt.

Knowing he could never beat his sense of duty, Sigurbjörn grabbed the phone before it fell on the floor and answered it. "This is Sigurbjörn."

Guilty apprehension filled Ingimundur's gravelly voice: "Ah, Siggi? I'm glad I caught you. You weren't sleeping, were you?"

Sigurbjörn had worked a brutal shift at the hospital in Selfoss earlier that day. The drive home to his little apartment complex in Vík had been dreadful as well, the graying clouds that engulfed the sky heralding a bad weather. Thinking nothing of it during his commute, he had crashed on the bed as soon as he had stepped inside. "No, not at all. What´s up?"

A disgruntled sigh was heard on the other end. "Well, we got a call from the hotel at Vík, saying that two of their guests haven't reported back from their trip at Sólheimasandur beach."

Sigurbjörn rubbed his forehead as he shook his head. *Ding, ding, ding. We have a winner, Johnny.* "You mean at the plane wreckage? Did they get lost or something?"

Ingimundur, the head of Víkverji, shared Sigurbjörn's views on hapless tourists and let out a mirthless chuckle. "I know it's a far-fetched idea to go out there in the middle of the night, but anything can happen with travelers, of course. But the thing is, the weather forecast said it'd be pretty bad tonight, and well, I think it got worse than their predictions."

"Really?" Sigurbjörn scrambled out of bed and shuffled toward the window across his room. He pulled the curtain back and swore.

Sleet obscured half his window. The tires of his little Suzuki Jimny were buried in thick snow while the other small cars were in an even sorrier state. White, wet flakes flew across the obsidian sky, carried away by the howling wind.

"I thought you knew," Ingimundur said, laughing. "I guess I did wake you, then."

Sigurbjörn hated lying to his fellow SAR, even when it was as simple as lying about being asleep. "Sorry, but I'm up now. How many do you need for the operation?"

"I've already called Fannar and he's going to meet you at the garage. I couldn't reach the others."

Well, it is *eleven at night,* Sigurbjörn thought. All of them were volunteers and if they could manage to get time away from working in these conditions, they did. Especially when most of them were either young students or family people. He opened his closet to find his woolen underwear. He was going to need it. "Don't worry about it. I'll see if I can rouse anyone."

After saying good bye to Ingimundur and putting on his SAR winter overalls, Sigurbjörn gazed out the window. He couldn't help frowning at the weather. He was going to need to bribe them with a six pack and a pizza party to get them to set foot in the hideousness that was the Icelandic winter.

Chapter 2: The Troop

Exhaustion shrouded the eyes of the only two people Sigurbjörn managed to pull out of bed. Snædís, the most experienced hiker in their group, yawned as she wobbled into the SAR building. She kept her fine, flyaway hair in a tight ponytail with a fleece headband.

Torfi, the youngest and latest volunteer, swiveled in the desk chair, his eyes glassy and out of focus. He'd told Sigurbjörn he'd been gaming most of the evening and needed some fresh air to clear out his head.

Sigurbjörn would never say it out loud, but if he could pick whoever he wanted for his troop, he'd get someone who was more experienced in winter retrievals. But then again, Torfi needed the training and this expedition would be a standard tourist rescue.

"Thank you for coming on such short notice."

"Is it just going to be us?" Snædís asked.

Sigurbjörn shook his head. "No, Fannar will be here shortly."

Snædís's shoulders tensed. She turned away, but Sigurbjörn caught her rolling her eyes and muttering, "Great."

"Where are we going? Up on the glacier?" Torfi asked as he swiveled toward the half-obscured window.

"God, I hope not," Snædís said. "What idiots would venture up there in this weather?"

Sigurbjörn gave her a knowing smirk. Her lips twitched. They had both been volunteers long enough to know there existed all kinds of idiots. "Don't worry. We're going to the beach for some sun and tan."

Both Snædís and Torfi frowned. Sigurbjörn's grin withered. People never appreciated his jokes. He cleared his throat. "Some tourists are lost near the plane wreck on Sólheimasandur, so we're going to pick them up. Grab the blankets and LED headlamps."

Torfi pulled himself up from the chair with a groan and shuffled to the shelves where they kept the extra woolen blankets. Sigurbjörn went into the kitchen and made a steaming pot of coffee, making it as black and bitter as possible, since that was how Fannar liked it.

"What car are we taking?" Snædís asked, and looked around at the absence of cars in the garage. "I thought the Land Rover was in the shop, and Ingimundur had the Ford 150 over in Kirkjubæjarklaustur."

Sigurbjörn grimaced at the bitter taste of the coffee before he nodded. "We're going in Fannar's SUV."

Snædís scowled. "That old thing?"

As if her comment had summoned the vehicle, the garage door creaked open and let in a flurry of wet snow that hit the linoleum floor. A huge, gray Nissan Patrol rolled in with a roar. After turning off the engine, Fannar stepped out. Big and stocky, his sunburned, wrinkly face was underlined in auburn beard. He smacked his hands together and let out a raucous laugh. "How are we feeling this fine night? Feeling fresh?" When he spotted Snædís, his smile grew bigger. "Ready for a nice little hike together, sweetheart?"

Snædís rolled her eyes with a frown and kept her distance, her arms crossed on her chest.

Torfi snickered and put the headlamps, blankets and flares into the Nissan's trunk.

Chuckling and without waiting for a reply, Fannar proceeded to grab a cup of coffee. He took a huge gulp of the steaming liquid, his jowls quivering. "Well, I don't know about you, but I'm ready to give those tourists a good lecture."

He slapped Sigurbjörn on the arm with grating laughter and poured the rest of the bean juice into two large thermoses. If the tourists were cold, the SAR usually offered them coffee or hot chocolate. Fannar's coffee could make them run for the hills, however, so Sigurbjörn prepared another batch, just in case. He was all for educating the tourists, not torturing them.

As Sigurbjörn was letting Fannar in on the instructions and route, he heard Snædís gasp when she opened the passenger door.

"What's a rifle doing here?" she demanded and pointed at the weapon nestled between the seats, its barrel pointing to the ceiling of the jeep.

Fannar waved her off. "It's just my hunting rifle. No big deal, sweetheart."

"I've told you to stop calling me that. And besides, hunting season ended a month ago," Snædís said, narrowing her eyes. "Are you hunting illegally?"

Fannar scoffed. "Of course not. I'm keeping it in the car because the missus doesn't want it in our house."

Snædís stepped away from the SUV and put her hands on her hips. "Well, I don't want it anywhere near me while we're on the road. What if we hit a pothole and the rifle goes off?"

Fannar threw back his head in laughter. "Ain't gonna happen, my dear. Unless, of course, *you* would start handling it. But never fear; I'm a gentleman. I'll keep it in the trunk with the safety on and everything."

He made a show of bowing sarcastically to Snædís as he grabbed the rifle and shoved it between the pile of blankets and other junk he hadn't bothered to clear away before arriving.

Snædís glared at Sigurbjörn, as if saying it was his fault that Fannar was an eccentric old man who was pretty much set in his ways. He knew they didn't get along, but there wasn't much that he could do. Fannar didn't like taking orders or scolding from someone younger than him. Sigurbjörn could only shrug and mouth, "bear with it."

As they got dressed in their SAR winter gear, with Snædís shooting a disgruntled glare at Fannar, and Torfi still breaking free of last night's gaming stream, Sigurbjörn's dread began to seep into his bones.

Adding the animosity between his teammates and the horrid weather conditions, he had a feeling it was going to be a bumpy ride.

Chapter 3: The Trek

he Icelandic ring road was known for its smooth asphalt running around the country. Old convertibles and SUVs had no problem driving through that road and people barely felt the ground underneath.

Such was not the case with Fannar's old Nissan Patrol. The vehicle ricocheted and vibrated like a broken jackhammer, its huge tires bumping into its frame.

Snædís held on to the roof handle for dear life; all color drained out of her face. A sickly, green hue gradually came over her.

Torfi was conked out. The energy drink he'd consumed before they set out apparently had the opposite effect. No amount of bumps his forehead got from the window stirred him from his sleep.

Sigurbjörn was used to rough driving, having grown up trekking on the glaciers with his father. Allowing the shakes of his seat to settle on his body, it brought forth pleasant memories. The abysmal weather even added a nice sprinkle to his walk down memory lane. It reminded him that despite the weather conditions, he was born to help people, whether in the hospital or out there risking his life in the unpredictable cold.

The windshield wipers squeaked as they struggled to keep the sleet away from the front. Fannar sucked air between his teeth and squinted against the darkness. The headlights of the SUV barely managed to cut through it. "I hope those goddamn tourists found shelter in this weather."

Sigurbjörn nodded. "I hope so too, but the only thing big enough on Sólheimasandur is the wreckage itself."

Fannar grunted. "It's such a stupid tourist spot. When I was little, people didn't care about that thing. It was just an unfortunate accident that the government couldn't afford to remove at the time. Now it's suddenly a hot spot for annoying 'influencers'." He air quoted the last word with disdain.

"Well, if it wasn't for those influencers, our economy wouldn't be booming," Snædís pointed out through gritted teeth.

Sigurbjörn glanced at her through the side-view mirror. The green hue was getting darker. He was grateful that she opened the window and breathed in long and slow to quell her queasiness. Snædís had a point, though. As much as it got on everyone's nerves when it came to tourists and their reckless ways, Icelanders had to thank tourism for keeping the country afloat. Whether it was a good thing or a bad thing, it certainly kept Sigurbjörn and his crew busy most of the year.

"This specific place is getting ridiculous, though," Fannar said.

Snædís brushed snow from the tip of the window before rolling it back up. "What do you mean? How is it any different than the other places?"

"Well, for one thing, this isn't the first time people have gone missing down there."

Sigurbjörn frowned. "Wait, really?"

"Two months ago, a French couple disappeared near the wreckage. It was on the news and everything," Fannar said.

Sigurbjörn's brows scrunched up together as he struggled to remember. Hadn't he been on vacation in Tenerife with his buddies around that time? Oh, how he wished he were there right now, soaking up that blessed vitamin D. He shrugged. "I don't remember that, to be honest. In fact, I don't think I was even in the country. Were they ever found?"

Fannar gave him a grim chuckle. "Not even a shred of hair was found. Maybe they got too close to the ocean and a rip tide snatched them. Ingimundur told me he thought he saw something protruding from the sand, but whatever it was, the Earth already claimed it. Like it always does, eventually."

That possibility wasn't that far-fetched. In fact, while Sigurbjörn didn't remember reading about that French couple, his memory projected a Spanish couple that had disappeared during a stormy night reminiscent of this, and how he and his fellow teammates had found their still bodies in the sand the next day. He remembered the pale faces marred from the storm, the way their rigid bodies curled up in the fetal position, as if it could have protected them from the elements. How badly dressed they had been for the trek. The woman, in particular, had been clutching her belly. Snædís had told him later on, with a mournful look on her face, that autopsy results had revealed the woman had been eight weeks pregnant. What a horrible way to go, for all of them. Regret gripped his insides with razor-sharp claws. He knew he shouldn't feel like that, yet it happened every once in a while whenever he witnessed a child accident, or worse, death, in the hospital. Every time, he wished he could have done something, *anything*, to make the ones afflicted feel less sorrow. But there was nothing he could have done. He let out a sigh. Sigurbjörn wasn't the praying type, but he hoped death wouldn't be the case for the tourists they were tasked to find.

"I hope it won't end up being a cadaver search," Snædís muttered distressed, mirroring Sigurbjörn's thoughts and memories. "I don't want to discover another body."

"Don't worry, it won't come to that," Fannar said as he glanced at her through the rear-view mirror. "We'll give the search a few hours, and if the weather worsens by then or if we haven't found them by that time, we'll have to try again tom—"

A screech erupted from below the Nissan, followed by a sharp cut.

Fannar swore and pumped the brakes. The SUV swerved dangerously on the icy sand. Panic hit Sigurbjörn in the gut and he gripped the roof handle until his knuckles numbed from the strength. Snædís shrieked and Torfi woke up with a startled yelp.

Out of the inky blackness, Sigurbjörn could see a huge shape approaching faster and closer.

"Fannar, look out!" he screamed and squeezed his eyes shut, awaiting the harsh and painful impact.

"I see it," Fannar growled through gritted teeth. He turned the wheel sharply to the left. The SUV pivoted in a half circle; snow and sand flurried in a hellish maelstrom. It hit the windows with the force of bullets, shattering the one in the back.

Torfi could only blink in shocked stupor before Snædís pulled him down. Snædís's shrieks muffled as she covered their faces with a blanket to protect against the glass fragments.

The vehicle came to a crashing halt in the end as its side slammed into the front of the plane wreckage.

CHAPTER 4: WHAT CAUSED THE CRASH

igurbjörn awoke in a coughing fit after his head had rammed against the passenger window. A crushing headache came in waves as he groaned.

"Is everyone okay?" he called, the volume of his own voice grinding against his skull. "Snædís? Torfi?"

A whimper came from Torfi who was shaking like a popcorn bag. Snædís winced when she carefully raised her head and shook off fragments of shattered glass. Fannar was slumped on the wheel, a thin rivulet of blood trickling down his right temple.

"Shit," Sigurbjörn muttered, clambering next to the old man. He pushed his forefinger and middle finger below Fannar's jaw. There was a pulse. A steady one. Sigurbjörn let out the breath he'd been holding in.

"Is he?" Snædís asked loudly over the forceful gale that barged through the broken window.

"He's fine. Just knocked out cold," Sigurbjörn yelled. Bitter chill seeped into his flesh. He shivered and pulled out from his backpack a large woolen scarf his grandmother had knitted for him. He wrapped it twice around his bruised neck and the scratchy warmth settled against his bare skin. He then carefully positioned Fannar so that his head rested against the door.

"What did we hit?" Snædís asked while she was busy with taping one of the blankets to the broken window at the back.

Sigurbjörn shrugged. "I have no idea. Probably a rock or something."

Snædís huffed. "Must have been a big fucking rock. Do you think the Nissan is in working condition?"

"Only one way to find out," Sigurbjörn grunted as he braced himself for the biting wind and opened the passenger door.

The blizzard pushed back with such ferocity, Sigurbjörn worried he might slam the door on his own fingers. He eventually won that round of tug-o-war the second the weather sucked in its breath and he stumbled out of the car.

Sleet blurred his vision. Sigurbjörn groped the SUV's exterior for both balance and to check for heavy damage. When he came around to the back, his sleeve caught onto something in the massive tire. He leaned forward for a closer look, eyebrows scrunched together. It was too dark to properly tell, but the surface of the object was both smooth and piercing. Air leaked out of the rubber with a hiss through multiple places from where sharp rocks protruded. He wiggled one of them out of the tire, careful not to grasp the edges. He trudged back to the front of the Nissan and climbed into the passenger seat with a groan.

"Well?" Snædís asked immediately, pushing a cup of hot chocolate into Torfi's trembling hands. The boy was pale. His eyes shone with apprehensive fear.

"The left tire on the back is busted," Sigurbjörn said as he wiped wet snow from his beanie and scarf.

Snædís scoffed. "How is that possible?"

"Don't know, but I found this embedded in it," Sigurbjörn said as he opened his palm.

Frowning, Snædís grabbed one of the LED headlamps and switched it on. Bathed in the harsh, white light, it did little to reveal what the object was. Sigurbjörn turned it over in his hands, and saw a pearlescent sheen on the oblong shape.

"Wait, is that—" Snædís snatched it up and glared at it. "Is that a *shell?*"

Now that she said it, it *did* have that shiny-yet-brittle-looking feature of a shell, but the shape and size of it was all wrong. It was bigger and sharper than any shell he'd ever seen.

"How can a shell puncture a tire?" Snædís asked.

"Maybe it's a fossilized one?" Torfi offered, his voice raspy from not speaking since the departure.

Snædís tried breaking it in two with her hands, but to no avail. She passed it on to Sigurbjörn who attempted to smack it on his knee, but unfortunately it only caused him throbbing pain.

"Torfi might be right," Sigurbjörn muttered and rubbed his aching knee.

"I've never seen a shell this sharp, though," Snædís said as she ran a gloved finger along the edges. When she withdrew it, the knitted material had been cut cleanly. "Maybe the salt from the sea polished the edges?"

"It doesn't matter. We need to hurry up and start looking for the tourists. They could be hurt because of those things," Sigurbjörn said and carefully slipped the shell into his coat pocket. He could go to the Museum of National History and have it checked out later in the week. Who knows, maybe it was valuable.

"But how are we going to get around outside?" Torfi asked and gazed out the window, fleeting flecks of snow already melting on the glass. "The weather seems to be getting worse."

"We wrap ropes around our waists and tie the end to the hook of the Nissan. That way we won't get lost and we won't lose each other," Sigurbjörn said, and hoped Fannar had had the sense to bring some with them. "Now, let's gear up."

As Torfi and Snædís put on headlamps and ski goggles, Fannar roused with a painful grunt. Relief flooded Sigurbjörn. He was glad his friend was all right.

"What the hell happened?" the old man asked as he gingerly touched his bleeding temple.

Sigurbjörn filled him in while tying the rope Snædís found in the back of the trunk around his waist.

Fannar cursed loudly. "Well, that's just perfect. I had just finished my payments to the damn thing and getting a busted tire in the middle of nowhere during a fucking blizzard is not going to help with the insurance!"

"Do you want me to call for backup?" Sigurbjörn asked, despite knowing Fannar would never accept it. Old guys like him would never want to accept defeat like that.

"What? Hell no! I'll be fine. I've got a spare lodged on the trunk door. But there's no fucking way I can change it by myself in this weather."

Sigurbjörn almost volunteered to help, but stopped himself. If he stayed here with Fannar, that would leave Snædís alone with Torfi to do the search. Snædís was a good SAR, but she didn't have enough experience in these weather conditions. And Torfi was a complete beginner. Leaving Snædís with Fannar didn't bode well because she'd probably end up killing him if she got sick of his casual misogynistic behavior. No, Sigurbjörn needed an experienced member who knew what to expect if things got hard.

"Torfi, you'll stay here with Fannar and help him change the tire."

Torfi looked from the old man, to the gaping, howling chasm outside and nodded eagerly.

Sigurbjörn didn't blame him. He'd give anything to stay in the warmth of the car.

But duty called.

And the search began.

Chapter 5: The Search

Sigurbjörn regretted his decision five minutes after he'd stepped out of the vehicle.

Wet snow soaked his scarf as he and Snædís made the arduous trek around the wreckage. They tried calling in both English and Icelandic. They turned the flashlights on and off near the body of the plane to see if they caught any movement inside, but nothing but darkness greeted them. There was nothing else in the vicinity. They had no other choice but to scope out the area near the sea. Maybe the tourists thought they could get better shelter from the cliffs that sprouted on each side of the beach.

Water dripped down Sigurbjörn's spine with each breath he took. He made a promise to himself to take an hour-long bath once he returned home, followed with a tall glass of whiskey, hangover or sore body be damned. Irritation already prickling his skin, he wiped sleet from his goggles for the umpteenth time and stared hard at the frozen sand.

Dozens of footprints littered the ground, no doubt from tourists that came to see the wreckage, but Sigurbjörn couldn't discern if they were fresh or old ones.

"*Andskotinn*," he cursed and looked over his shoulder.

Snædís was still behind him, back bent and head rotating west and east, trying, just like him, to find prints that belonged to the missing tourists.

"Find anything?" he bellowed as loud as he could, though the blizzard swallowed most of it.

Snædís straightened and shook her head. "It's like finding a teardrop in the ocean, Siggi. I'm afraid we have to call it a night and try again tomorrow."

Sigurbjörn gritted his teeth. Deep down, that's what he wanted to do, but what if the tourists had found refuge near the shores and were just waiting for them to come and find them? If he left now and he'd read in the news the next morning that they'd frozen to death, it would have been his fault. He couldn't live with that. Not again.

"Let's walk a few more meters, just to be sure," he yelled and gave the rope a tug.

He heard a loud groan from behind him as they continued their search. Whether Snædís had the same sense of duty as he did or not, Sigurbjörn appreciated her company nonetheless. It made the search less lonely and bleak amid this howling oblivion.

After about a fifteen-minute trek, Sigurbjörn's clothes were wet from both the continuous sleet and his own sweat. He felt like they had been walking in circles, even though he knew the area quite well. Despite being in adequate shape, his knees ached from walking in the uneven frozen terrain. His ears rang from the shrieking wind and the crashing waves on the dark horizon. Numbness clutched his fingers and wouldn't let go. Vertigo threatened to overtake him after seeing nothing but hazy void. The flashlight he gripped in his hand showed no signs of life, no matter how far the beam reached. There were moments he thought he saw a shape out in the distance, but once they got closer, it was gone.

A trick of the light, or perhaps I've just been hallucinating, Sigurbjörn thought.

He paused in his walk. He heard a strange tinkling sound about thirteen meters to his left. Was it someone's phone? Was it a sign from the tourists, a beacon of some sort to let them know where they were? He strained his ears amid the furious gale, desperate to catch that sound again.

Nothing.

Whatever it had been, the storm had swallowed it. Sigurbjörn hung his head. The disappointment burned a hole in his motivation.

"Siggi, we have to go back," Snædís yelled as Sigurbjörn stooped down to see if any phones were buried in the sand. "I know you want to find them, but it's impossible. We should go back and help Fannar with the car."

She patted his already drenched back. Clenching his fists full of crunchy sand, he sighed in defeat. Again, the weather had gotten him beat. If there had been more people to help with the search, maybe it would have been successful. His head filled with 'what ifs' and 'maybes' that turned solid with guilt in his stomach.

We did all we could, given the circumstances, he thought miserably and made to stand up.

Something fluttered in the wind. Sigurbjörn blinked, afraid it had been a particularly long line of snow. He turned to the left, squinting against the barrage of snow that attacked his visage.

There it was again!

Something that reflected against the flashlight.

"Snædís, wait!" he yelled when the rope around his waist tugged impatiently. "I think I found something!"

Chapter 6: The Discovery

igurbjörn's heart raced. Not from exertion, but from hope that they might have found the tourists. It gave him an extra adrenaline rush as he bounced toward the object, pulling Snædís along with him.

The more the flashlight shone on it, the clearer it got. It was a neon pink backpack with a few cutesy-looking patches, such as Hello Kitty and Pikachu, sewn into it that made him think it belonged to a child. The backpack's straps fluttered wildly in the storm.

Sigurbjörn's elation deflated. He had hoped to see at least one of the tourists huddled in a hole with the backpack.

Snædís came wheezing next to him. She lowered her balaclava from her mouth and nose and frowned. "That's it?"

"It could mean they're not far away from here," Sigurbjörn pointed out, hearing the disappointment in her voice.

"You better hope they're close by," she grumbled and knelt to pick up the backpack, wrinkling her nose at the patches. She paused and turned the bag over. "Siggi?"

"What is it?" Sigurbjörn crouched beside her and shone the light on the bag. His wide eyes met hers.

The backpack was ripped to shreds on the front side. Ribbons of polyester flapped in the roaring wind, eager to be released from the remains. Empty chocolate bar wrappers tumbled out of the rifts and the weather snatched them away.

"What do you think happened?" Snædís asked.

Sigurbjörn's stomach plummeted. His flashlight had revealed a dark trail that had been hiding under the backpack. Splotches of blood were barely visible through the wet snow. He hadn't noticed it on the way because he had been so excited to find *something.*

"Shit, is that what I think it is?" Snædís asked as she leaned forward for closer examination.

Sigurbjörn didn't need to. His years working at the hospital had unfortunately made his nose super sensitive to the smell of blood. Even standing there in the middle of a raging blizzard, trickles of the iron stench found its way up his nostrils. Swallowing hard, Sigurbjörn led the beam ahead. The trail seemed to go toward the wreckage until it stopped at a crumpled heap.

He leapt up and broke into a jog, with Snædís close on his heels. Their years as volunteers kicked in. They needed to be ready to give first aid to the injured tourist. How he or she had gotten injured was a mystery to Sigurbjörn. There was nothing here, just a black wasteland with a destroyed plane. Unless the tourist had slipped on ice and cracked their head? There were no large enough stones protruding from the earth, though. Sigurbjörn shook off the thoughts racing in his mind. Once they had gotten the tourist off to safety, he could ask them.

The heap grew bigger as they approached. It was no wonder they hadn't seen it. A thick coating of snow already encapsulated it. The ground was dark around it. Darker and wetter than sand usually was at that time of year.

The smell hit him first. Sigurbjörn grabbed Snædís's arm and pulled her to a halt. Bile rose in his throat.

"What's wrong?" she asked.

Sigurbjörn didn't dare open his mouth, in fear of vomiting all over himself. He could only point a shaking finger.

Furrowing her brows, Snædís turned to where he was pointing. All color drained from her face. They had found the tourist. What was left of him, at least.

Blood had pooled around the thin, mangled body of a young Asian man. It was missing an arm and a leg. The limbs remaining were clad in simple jeans and a puffer jacket. Definitely not warm enough for Iceland's unpredictable weather. Even though the snow tried its best to conceal the brutality of that tourist's fate, Sigurbjörn could clearly see the pink guts and other pulpy viscera from the torn-out stomach.

Snædís turned around and retched.

Sigurbjörn repaid her the favor by patting her on the back as she hacked and coughed. He had witnessed death plenty of times at the hospital, but he had never encountered one so gruesome.

"What the fuck is this?" Snædís asked, voice raspy. She kept her back to the corpse.

Sigurbjörn shook his head, not able to peel his gaze away from the gore. There were chunks missing on some parts of the body, as if bitten or ripped off. The wounds shone raw in the flashlight.

"No, really, Siggi, what could have done *this*?" Snædís demanded.

"I don't know," he said, not surprised his own voice had gone hoarse.

"We need to call the police, or fuck, even animal control or something."

"Do you think an animal did this? There are no animals capable of this kind of slaughter in Iceland," Sigurbjörn said, but he wondered if certain people could. His mind traveled to dark regions where serial killers and zombies roamed the premises. He promptly shook it off. Zombies weren't real and the only serial killer Iceland had had lived centuries ago. Good luck to any maniac who'd thought he could escape this hell of an island.

"How the fuck should I know? Maybe a polar bear came on an iceberg or something," said Snædís, who began trudging back to the SUV, giving the body a wide berth.

Sigurbjörn mulled that over. It's true that an occasional polar bear ended up on Iceland's shore from time to time, but they usually showed up on the north side of the island. Furthermore, they would get swiftly taken down as soon as they set their paws on land. However, if that was the case, then they were in deep shit. What was the saying again? *If it's brown, lay down. If it's black, fight back. If it's white, good night.* Snædís was right. They needed to get back to town and get reinforcement.

A roar that cut through the wind curdled Sigurbjörn's blood. A sound he never expected to hear on the black beach.

Chapter 7: The Creature

"Holy shit! What was that?" Snædís yelled, her eyes wide behind the visors.

Sigurbjörn's feet sprouted roots, anchoring him to the ground. His heart pounded so hard his rib cage began to ache. Cold sweat gathered in his armpits. He had never heard a roar like that before. It sounded like a mix between a bear and the screech of glass clashing together. It cut through eardrums and left a bloody mess.

A few seconds later, another scream pierced the storm.

A human one.

"Fuck, it's Torfi," Snædís cursed, and then untied the rope and took off, her stomps crunching the frozen sand.

What sounded like cannon fire blasted through the blizzard and a crash followed. *Fannar must be using the rifle,* Sigurbjörn thought. He glanced down at the mutilated body. If he didn't hurry and help, they could all end up like that corpse. It was his duty as SAR to help people in trouble in any way possible. But no matter how much his mind willed him to run, his body wouldn't obey. If it *was* a polar bear attacking the group, he wouldn't stand a chance charging straight at it without any weapons. There was a reason for the saying, after all. Right now, all he wanted to do was to turn around and flee in the opposite direction, away from what danger awaited him by the wreckage.

He grabbed the arm that held the flashlight to stop himself from shaking. *Calm down,* he thought and clenched his jaws. *Your crew needs your help. You can't abandon them. They wouldn't do that to you if they were in your shoes. So, snap the fuck out of it and get moving!*

Clenching his fists and drawing a deep breath, Sigurbjörn ran after Snædís, following the bouncing light that twinkled amid the hail of snow.

After a minute or two, the light vanished.

"*Andskotinn,*" Sigurbjörn muttered, but kept running in the same direction. He almost wanted to shout to Snædís to pinpoint her location when he noticed how quiet it had become.

No more shots fired. The roaring had ceased as well. Only the buzz of the storm rang in his ears. He looked around to see if he saw any of the stripy patterns on Snædís's winter overalls reflecting from his flashlight. The area seemed deserted. The beam couldn't even detect the SUV or the wreckage through the storm. Had they all fled on their feet?

His foot tripped over something bulky in the sand. Flailing, he hit the ground stomach first. All air punched out of him. Inhaling tiny crystals of snow, Sigurbjörn turned to the side and cast a beam over the thing that had tripped him.

His insides lurched.

The warm light illuminated a leg torn from the knee. It was dressed in the red and blue winter overalls the SAR wore. A white sneaker, spattered with crimson, covered the foot. An ill-fitted choice to venture out in the cold environment of Iceland, but it was something only young people would do.

The beam caught sight of the rest of the body. His overalls glistened with fresh blood, steam rising from the ripped abdomen. His open, youthful eyes reflected no light. Snow was already gathered in his gaping mouth, as if desperately attempting to cover up the hideous murder.

Sigurbjörn pressed a gloved hand to his mouth to prevent himself from screaming. *Poor Torfi,* was all he could think. His mind played a cruel game where it showed him memories of the boy in training, his expression full of promise and hope.

A soft melody, reminiscent of a wind chime, tinkled close by. A deep thump reverberated in the solid earth. Sigurbjörn felt it travel to his bones. The tinkling grew stronger and clearer. Another thump followed. Closer this time. A horrible odor of rotten fish and blood stank up the air.

Sigurbjörn stayed still, barely allowing a breath to escape from his mouth. Whatever had killed the tourist and now Torfi was approaching. Had it already finished off Fannar and Snædís? Was that why he couldn't hear anything from them? And why was it emitting that strange sound? He wanted to turn off the flashlight that cast such a gruesome sight on Torfi, but he was afraid that could alert the thing that was lumbering over to his presence. Better to stay still and play statue.

Something snorted loudly. It reminded Sigurbjörn of horses, yet his mind conjured up a much more monstrous entity. Something with teeth and claws sharp enough to rip a person in two.

A furry front leg stomped next to Torfi's head. The tinkling pierced Sigurbjörn's ears. He ground his teeth. It sounded like crushed glass scraping up against concrete.

Sigurbjörn shifted ever so slightly to wipe the sleet from his goggles. He blinked rapidly, thinking whatever he saw in front of him was something the storm was conjuring up in preparation for his hypothermia.

The creature stopped by Torfi's head and sniffed his wet, snow-covered hair. Its head was similar to a bear's, though the snout was larger and wider. Yellowed, jagged teeth jutted out from its drooling mouth. The rest of its body was incomprehensible to Sigurbjörn. Thousands of pearlescent shells covered every inch of its bear-like body, with tiny fractions of brown fur sticking out where a shell or two was missing. They glittered in the light. Elongated, curved claws, reminiscent of sloths, scratched at the snow.

What kind of a beast was that? Sigurbjörn had never seen anything like that before. His mind went into overdrive. *Was it a new species? Something the pharmaceutical labs had cooked up? A failed military experiment, created to protect our land, gone awry?*

It could be all those possibilities, but one question burned brightest in Sigurbjörn's mind: could it be killed? Most likely. All creatures of nature have a weakness.

He watched in horrified silence as the monster buried its head into Torfi's open cavity and munched on the innards. Pink bits of intestines smeared around its mouth. Sigurbjörn heard the tinkling sound as it moved slightly to burrow deeper into Torfi's body. He realized it came from the shells covering its massive hide as they scraped together every time it moved. More of those shells protected the top of its head. A bullet to the head was not going to cut it. Sigurbjörn remembered the blast earlier, and was sure Fannar had tried it to no avail. Black soot on its crown was further proof of that.

Cramps were threatening to seize Sigurbjörn's arm. He gritted his teeth. How the hell could he get away without being seen by that creature? A clunky shadow loomed behind the monster as the storm eased up for a second. There were no lights near, but he surmised either the wreckage or the SUV weren't so far away. He could make a break for it and seek shelter in either of them. It was a far better option than being a possible dessert for that thing.

Sigurbjörn prayed it wasn't nocturnal as his fingers fumbled for the off switch on his LED headlamp. His other thumb was ready on the flashlight. He silently counted to three before casting himself and the monster in total darkness.

Despite the hail, Sigurbjörn heard the chimes as the creature raised its head from Torfi's corpse. It sniffed the air. Sigurbjörn imagined it looking in all directions, to see if it could catch the stench of fear already permeating from his skin. He had slowly risen to his knees, ready to sprint. If it could just *fucking turn* in the other direction. Growls issued from its throat.

Heavy steps thumped closer to Sigurbjörn. The shells jingled in tandem. Warm iron stink flitted toward him. He pressed his lips together, afraid he'd gag at the putrid odor. That thing panted a few meters from him; its claws sweeping the frozen ground, like a fishing net capturing fish hiding in the sandy bottom of the sea. Sigurbjörn could smell a mixture of seaweed, rotten fish and Torfi's guts coming from its mouth.

It was over. There was no way he could run away from those long, strong legs. Who was he kidding earlier about being in adequate shape? His stamina had always been crap. Sigurbjörn's ball sack shriveled as the warmth of the creature, with its raspy panting, approached him.

He squeezed his eyes shut. He didn't want the visage of that monster to be the last thing he saw in his death. The goddamn tinkling would haunt him in the afterlife. He forced his mind to show a reel of his mother and father, both safe in Reykjavík, not having a clue what was about to befall their only son. His whole body trembled along with the deep thumps of the monster.

A blast of red light overpowered the inky darkness of his shut eyes.

The creature roared. The sound nearly exploded Sigurbjörn's eardrums at such close proximity.

"Siggi! Get over here!"

He barely heard Snædís's commanding scream through the ringing of his ears. It sparked something in him, though.

Hope.

Sigurbjörn opened his eyes. Through the wet sleet on his goggles, he saw Snædís standing about ten meters from the monster, waving a lit flare in big, half circles. It reminded him of Dr. Alan Grant from *Jurassic Park*. He almost burst out loud laughing at Snædís's insane bravery.

The creature backed away from the flare, growling and spitting thick, viscous drool. Out of the corner of his eye, Sigurbjörn detected another movement from under the Nissan.

Fannar, his leg badly injured, crawled by one of the tires, his other arm clutching his rifle. Blood smeared half his face, matting his beard and obscuring his sight. He tried aiming the barrel toward the creature, but his elbows buckled and collapsed under his weight.

The bear-like cryptid stood on its hind legs and bellowed another fear-inducing roar. It bent its front legs and swiped at Snædís with its massive claws. She turned and threw herself down into the ground, the claws ripping into her overalls. She let out a painful yowl and dropped the flare.

Sigurbjörn couldn't hesitate any longer. Ignoring the ache in his knees, he sprinted toward Fannar, looking over his shoulder in case the monster gave chase. To his horror, it was much more interested in taking down Snædís and the red-hot flare. Panting, he slid under the vehicle and positioned himself next to the old man.

"Glad you're alive, kid," Fannar coughed. A speckle of blood pattered the snow.

Sigurbjörn didn't like the way the old man looked. "How bad is it?" he asked, already wondering if Fannar had packed his first aid kit in the trunk.

Fannar grimaced in pain. "That thing got my leg with its nasty claws when I had finished putting the tire on. I hit my head on the busted one, which gave me this." He gestured to his bloody face. "Thankfully, Torfi tossed the rifle to me, I got a shot at it, but that didn't do much. I managed to climb into the car and lock the driver's door. Poor Torfi got so scared of being crushed within the car that he clambered out and tried to run for it." He jerked his head toward the body. "You saw how that got him."

Sigurbjörn nodded grimly. Torfi's brutal murder would unfortunately take up permanent residence in his head for years to come. He took Fannar's rifle from his stiff fingers.

"What are you doing?" he demanded and groped for the handle.

"No offense, Fannar, but you could accidentally hit Snædís in your condition."

Fannar frowned as he pushed the case of bullets to Sigurbjörn. "You got any experience shooting?"

He glanced at the weapon. It was something he would use in video games, but in real life? Sigurbjörn slid a few rounds into the chamber and pumped. "Only one way to find out."

Chapter 8: The Hunt

igurbjörn placed the tip of the rifle on a small rock. The weapon was heavier than he expected, or was it just the burden weighing down on him? He blew air from his puffed-out cheeks to stave off the nervous nausea.

Fannar helped him secure the butt of the rifle under his shoulder. "The recoil is a bitch, kiddo. Don't flinch and drop the gun."

Sigurbjörn nodded, already feeling a spasm below his clavicle. The shock of firing would also be intense, but he was prepared for it. He just hoped his soaked beanie would be enough to protect his ears.

Snædís was still fighting the monster by herself. She had lit another flare which created a small barrier between her and the beast. It seemed afraid of the flame as it kept growling and circling around her, a predator biding its time.

Snædís walked slowly backward, strands of her hair whipping her face, as she made her way to the shelter of the wreckage, her shrieks and yells carrying through the howling wind.

The beast's eyes narrowed, and it gave another thunderous roar. It went on all fours, bent its knees and charged toward Snædís.

"Now, you idiot, *now!*" Fannar yelled and shook Sigurbjörn's arm.

Gulping, Sigurbjörn wiped sleet from his forehead and goggles. Closing one eye, he took aim at one of the beast's legs. His finger, on the verge of cramping, squeezed the trigger.

The rifle's release of the bullet cut into Sigurbjörn's brain in a cacophony of explosions. He let out a startled yelp and almost dropped the gun.

The monster gave off a spine-tingling screech. He must have hit it. Smashed glass reverberated through the storm. It turned its head back, glaring at the SUV. It took one step backward, ready to attack the vehicle. The shells vibrated as its back arched, creating a sinister symphony of chimes.

Snædís used that opportunity to inch closer to the plane. Sensing her movement, the creature veered back to her, and with a snarl, resumed its chase. Snædís threw the flare with a scream at it and fumbled in her backpack for another marker. It bounced off the charging creature, but it did manage to startle it to a halt. It stomped the ground with its claws and bared its teeth at her. The tinkling of the shells turned darker, similar to conical flutes.

"It doesn't want Snædís near the wreckage," Fannar muttered.

"Do you think it's protecting it or something?" Sigurbjörn asked as he reloaded the rifle.

"Hell if I know," Fannar said. "Just keep shooting the damn thing!"

Scowling, Sigurbjörn positioned the rifle back on the rock, aimed once again at the creature's legs and pulled the trigger.

The bullet soared through the air and buried itself into the metal of the wreckage. A high-pitched squeak came from it. Sigurbjörn lowered the rifle. *What kind of sound was that?*

The beast stopped in its tracks. Panting, with steam drifting from its drooling mouth, it looked back toward the SUV. Its snout wrinkled in rage. The shells across its body vibrated more feverishly, as if getting ready to launch from its hide.

Sigurbjörn paled. He had never hunted before, but he knew a pissed-off look when he saw one. And that monster was *livid*.

"Oh, shit," he whispered and frantically shoved another bullet into the chamber.

The shell monster lowered its head, eyes piercing, before it released another T-Rex bellow. Its claws left deep indents in the frozen sand as it hurled itself at the Nissan.

"Fuck!" Fannar screamed, and pulled the rest of his body behind the tire, quivering in the fetal position and muttering prayers under his breath.

Teeth chattering, Sigurbjörn shot again. The bullet grazed one of the shells above the creature's back, not even breaking it. As it approached at an alarming speed, Sigurbjörn quickly flung himself behind the tire next to Fannar.

The ground shook violently as the beast body-slammed into the SUV. Glass shattered into a hundred pieces and rained down upon the snow, casting fractals of light in all directions. The old Nissan, thankfully, withstood the brute force of the creature, but Sigurbjörn realized it wouldn't hold for long. He fumbled around the snow for more bullets. His fingers clasped on one. He scanned the ground, his stomach plummeting.

It was the last bullet.

The SUV tilted precariously to the other side, almost exposing the two men. The metal creaked as the monster's claws dug into the vehicle. One more push or tackle from the beast and their shelter was no more.

It stood on its hind legs once more and pounded its massive paws on the hood of the SUV. The tires sunk into the sand.

Sigurbjörn dared to glance up at that exact moment. His eyes widened. The monster's belly was free from shells. Only matted brown fur protected its insides. There was its weakness. That was his chance! Having no idea whether it shared the same biology as a bear, Sigurbjörn threw caution to the wind and shoved himself directly underneath the animal, the rifle raised upward.

He let out a roar of his own and pulled the trigger. The flash almost blinded him. Blinking away stars that obscured his sight, he saw how much damage a rifle shot could make at point blank range.

Blood, tattered fur, and other viscera plopped down on his face and chest. The steaming warmth of it was awfully unsettling. The monster let out a whimpering wheeze as it backpedaled away from the SUV.

Groaning and spitting in disgust, Sigurbjörn wiped away the gore and scrambled to his feet, adrenaline fueling his limbs. Even with no bullets left, he was ready to hit it with the rifle in case it attacked once more.

"Jesus fucking Christ," Fannar muttered. "I think you got it."

The beast staggered a few steps and clawed at its open belly. It blinked its black eyes at Sigurbjörn, as if not believing a human could injure a force of nature like itself. It let out a gurgle before it collapsed a mere three meters from Torfi's body. The ground shook one last time as the body hit the sand.

"You can let go of the gun now, kid," Fannar said softly and attempted to pull the rifle from him.

Sigurbjörn didn't give in. He needed to wait a few minutes to be certain the creature was dead. If he had a huge rock, he would stumble over and smash it on its head until there was nothing left, but there were no such rocks in sight. Therefore, he had to make do with waiting.

Stomping footsteps jolted him back after staring at the inanimate carcass for what he thought had been eternity. Snædís stopped in front of the Nissan, breathing heavily.

"I'm so glad you're not hurt," Sigurbjörn said, relief swelling in his heart.

"Likewise." Snædís said, managing a smile in-between wheezing and coughing.

Together, they helped Fannar on his feet. He cursed bloody murder when he tried to put weight on his leg. The injury looked bad; ribbons of flesh hung from his leg, exposing raw tissue to the elements. It seemed the monster had taken a chunk from his calf as well.

"We need to get you to a hospital," Sigurbjörn said as he tried his best to bandage up Fannar's wounds. He realized his hands shook as he wrapped Fannar's leg in gauze. The aftermath of tackling the beast was taking over his body.

Fannar winced and nodded, his old tough man facade withering away from the pain. He rummaged through the first aid kit and popped three painkillers into his mouth. "Too bad it's not morphine," he grunted and nudged Sigurbjörn in the elbow.

Sigurbjörn shook his head, smiling. He hoped he'd get Fannar's weird positivity when he got older.

"I need to you show you something first," Snædís said to Sigurbjörn. "I-I found the other tourist."

Sigurbjörn wasn't sure if his nerves, or even his stomach, could handle another massacre. "I'm good. Let's just head back home."

Snædís grabbed his arm. Her eyes were wide with apprehension. "You *need* to see this, Siggi."

Sigurbjörn resisted the urge to scowl. He didn't know Snædís had such a morbid fascination with dead bodies. Maybe she needed another person to help identify the body. He glanced over his shoulder to check on Fannar. The old man waved them off and sat against the busted tire, his rifle resting on his lap.

Exhaustion took hold of Sigurbjörn's body once the adrenaline wore off. He wanted nothing more than to crash on his bed. His feet ached in his comfortable hiking boots and the bones in his fingers creaked every time he flexed them.

A high-pitched whimper pierced the silent trek toward the wreckage.

Sigurbjörn froze. His heart began doing jumping jacks once more. It was the same kind of sound he'd heard when one of his bullets hit the body of the plane.

"It's okay," Snædís said and kept walking until she disappeared into the hole of the wreckage.

Sigurbjörn took a deep breath. *It can't get any worse*, he thought as he bounced a little on his toes and then went in after her.

The old US Navy plane was barren on the inside. Every seat and gadgets had been stripped off after the crash in 1973, since that was the only thing people could carry at the time. The empty interior and the gaping holes for windows wouldn't have provided good shelter for the tourists, as the torrent barged into every open crevice.

Sigurbjörn spotted Snædís at the cockpit. The plane creaked as he ventured near. She looked over her shoulder, casting Sigurbjörn in harsh light before turning forward.

The light on her LED headlamp illuminated the sight before them.

A female tourist was there, that was for sure, but the state of the body was worse than of the male tourist, or Torfi's. Arms and legs had been torn off, clothes gone and picked clean of flesh. There was only chewed bones. The face was nearly unidentifiable—the eyes had been clawed out by small claws and the cheeks chewed off. Worse was the torso, as the rib cage was cracked open and empty. The culprits lay inside the cavity, gnawing on the jagged pieces of bones.

Sigurbjörn stared.

Three miniature versions of the monster he had just slayed hissed and growled at them. The shells on their bodies didn't seem as sturdy and they only covered a small portion of their backs. Sigurbjörn was no expert of monsters, but with the disappearance of the French couple, he estimated they were around two-month old.

"This is why it didn't want me to approach the plane," Snædís said, her nose wrinkling at the stench of death that permeated from the body and the cubs. "She was just protecting her babies."

"But *what* are they?" Sigurbjörn asked.

Snædís sighed. "Probably just a freak of nature. Iceland's full of them, you know?"

"What should we do? Should we kill them?"

Snædís turned startled eyes at Sigurbjörn. "They're just babies. Their mom probably needed to feed them and those poor tourists were there, ripe for their picking. It might have even taken the French couple too."

Sigurbjörn's blood chilled. That monster had already killed and eaten five people. If those things grew up to the same size as its mother, who knew how much havoc they could wreak? "Then what do you suggest we do, huh?"

Snædís looked back at the cubs. Her expression became somber. "Let nature deal with them. It's where they're from and it's how it should be."

Sigurbjörn glared at the cubs. They cowered and sought refuge within the corpse. They were harmless, for the moment, especially with no mother to protect them. Besides, he had no desire to kill them. He had already stained his hands with the death of their mother and that was enough for him. Dealing with the cubs wasn't as important as getting Fannar to the hospital.

"All right, we'll leave them alone tonight. But we need to alert the police and animal control about our findings."

Snædís nodded.

Together they backed away from the wreckage, their eyes trained on the future forces of nature that continued to nibble on the corpse

EPILOGUE

The location of the wreckage had been closed off until the storm receded. Sigurbjörn had notified the farmer who owned the land to keep an eye on any movement near the plane, but strongly advised him to *not* go there until the police came the next day. They did not need to find a sixth body over there.

He and Snædís had dreaded returning to the popular tourist spot to retrieve Torfi's body. They had contacted his family about their boy's fate, but had left out how he had died. Telling them it had been a tragic accident had been awful enough. The police would definitely have some questions for them in regards to the state of the body, but he'd have to worry about that later. He'd hoped the baby monsters hadn't gotten their clawed paws on it. As gruesome as it was to think it, he'd hoped the body of the female tourist would be plenty of food source for them.

Police and animal control kept them company along the way, bombarding them with questions, but the two of them refused to say anything until they arrived at the wreckage.

Seeing was believing, after all.

The plane glittered on the snow when they arrived. The busted tire was laid out a few meters from it along with indents on the sand from where the Nissan had sunk after the monster's attack. There were evidence of an attack, with blood on the ground and the sand disturbed. What they found, however, was Torfi's frozen body along with the remains of the tourists. The rest, the shell monster and its cubs, had vanished.

Sigurbjörn and Snædís looked everywhere, with the police men either retching on the ground or running back to their vehicles to retrieve body bags.

The creatures were nowhere to be found. It was as if they had never existed to begin with. Snædís stared hopelessly at Sigurbjörn. He knew she was wondering if they had gone insane, if the horrible state of the tourists' bodies had just tripped them up. How would that explain Torfi's murder, though?

He noticed something on the ground, though. Something large had been dragged through the sand. He followed the tracks silently, relieved to get away from the stench of vomit and the looming questions. They lead to the ocean, the waves lapping at his feet, as if beckoning him to pursue further.

Sigurbjörn sighed. "Smart bastards."

A winter gale pushed him closer to the waves. Shivering, he shoved his hands into his coat pocket. He winced at a sudden jab of pain that coursed from his finger. His eyes widened. He pulled out the shell from his pocket.

The only evidence of the shell monster that protected their landmark rested in the palm of his hand.

Notes from the Author

The Girl with The Hooves

Everyone in Iceland knows about Grýla. She is essentially Iceland's "boogeyman". She's always depicted as a huge monster that eats children, but I wanted to explore her origin, since there are no tales that I know of that speak of how she became this vicious troll that comes down from the mountains to hunt and eat naughty kids. I guess I have a soft spot for villains, as long as their origins resonate with me.

It was featured in the charity anthology, The Endless Dark Winter, edited by Martin W. Francis in 2020.

Survival of the Fittest

Iceland is one of those privileged countries that doesn't have to rely on nuclear power in order to receive electricity and heat.

So, it doesn't come as a surprise that I'm a little bit afraid of nuclear power and the toxic radioactivity it generates afterwards. When I lived in Japan in 2011, I felt the fear from the Japanese when the tsunami hit the Fukushima power plant. I've also seen bits and pieces of the objects that were left after the bombing of Hirashima and Nagasaki, and it left quite an impact on me. Seeing the photos of the devastation was horrendous and I never want anyone to experience it.

With the current wars happening in the world right now, I'm becoming more and more afraid that these nations will end up using their nuclear weapons.

And what's one of the advices I usually give to aspiring horror writers: Write what scares you.

However, with that in mind, I always wondered what immortal creatures, such as vampires, would do in these situations. Would they wander around the globe, searching for blood? Would they do anything to survive? Wouldn't you?

They Came From the Rocks

It was 2021. The Icelandic TV show *Katla* had just been released on Netflix and I was enthralled by it. In true Icelandic fashion, it was dark and bleak. There's one scene that involves a family with a troublesome child that lives rent free in my head (if you know, you know). The concept of doppelgangers or Huldufólk emerging from the volcano was fascinating to me and it was a great inspiration to this story.

Even though found footage horror is not one of my favorite horror genres to watch, I do enjoy experimenting with writing them. I was invited to Keith Anthony Baird's charity anthology *Hex-periments* and I thought this story was perfect for it.

While the TV show doesn't have the explicit message of the dangers of tampering with nature, I included it in my story. Because you should never fuck with nature. It can take care of itself.

Tupperware Party

This story is my tribute to slashers. You know the ones, like Friday the 13th and Halloween. They're not my favorite horror genres, but they're entertaining nonetheless.

It was featured in Kandisha Press' *Slash-Her A Women of Horror Anthology*, published in 2022.

When I saw the submission call to that anthology, I really wanted to submit to it, but I had no story. I had already done a serial killer story for the third volume of the *Women of Horror Anthology*, so I wanted to do something different but keeping in style with my revenge themes.

I've always been morbidly fascinated by cults and scam stories and I'd been watching a lot of MLM (Multi-Level Marketing) shows on

YouTube. I don't know what it is, but there's something about people being netted into these schemes and if they want to earn any kind of money, they're forced to sell these products to friends and family, ultimately becoming alienated by them.

That's when the idea for this story hit me. A balls-to-the-wall, ridiculously campy revenge slasher story with a Final Girl. I was grinning ear-to-ear the whole time I wrote it. I had so much fun with it.

You haven't seen the last of Martha. I'm cooking up a sequel to this story, which will be equally campy and ridiculous.

Hell of a Ride

I wish I could say I was adventurous, but as a person suffering from anxiety and who overthinks everything, I envy the ones who simply jump into action, carpe diem-style. I mean, the only bone I've ever broken is my toe and that was an embarrassing incident. Despite being cautious, I *do* enjoy consuming anything adventurous, whether it be tv shows, movies, listening to a friend's trip or reading about it.

That's why I was excited when Off Limits Press opened up submissions for their Far From Home: Adventure Horror Anthology. Doubts ran through me, though. There are so many talented horror writers out there. What if they won't pick my story? In the end, I decided to throw caution to the wind and actually *be* adventurous by submitting this story. The squeals of joy that reverberated throughout the apartment when they accepted it.

Most of the stories that include Icelandic monsters usually serve as a cautionary tale about the dangers of nature, but I wanted to include a small vengeful spirit in there for added spice.

It includes one of my favorite Icelandic monsters, Nykur. I love the kind of monsters who can blend into the environment seamlessly and I hope readers who decide to be adventurous and travel to Iceland, will from here on take a closer look at all the horses around.

ALL-YOU-CAN-DRINK BUFFET

I've studied the culture and the language of Japan at the University of Iceland. I was also lucky enough to be able to live there for two years. With a Bachelor's degree and a Master's degree in the subject, I often get asked why I don't work in Japan. Being raised in a country that values equal rights, I discovered that I would not thrive working in Japan for a long time. For one, I value having a good work-life balance and unfortunately, Japan still hasn't really incorporated that balance into their working environment. They're trying to change that, mind you, but for now it's tiny, teeny baby steps.

So, I imagine it must be hard for Westerners to adapt to the Japanese working regime, especially when they come from a culture that enforces or encourages individualism or independence. I wanted to showcase the struggle of trying to fit in a place where you stick out like a sore thumb.

I'm also a huge Junji Ito fan, so I was inspired by his weird horror stories and it would be a dream come true if he adapted my story into one of his mangas.

THE HAG'S GIFT

I consider myself a closeted witch. Like most girls, I had my witchy phase when I was a teenager, casting spells and buying crystals and topping it all off by watching *The Craft* and *Practical Magic*. Nowadays, I tend to stick reading about witchcraft and its interesting lore.

When Cemetery Gate*s Media announced its submissions to its* Campfire Macabre Vol. 1, I wanted to try to write a story about witchcraft, but, of course, make it Icelandic. I was so glad they enjoyed my Icelandic version of witchcraft as it was included in their anthology.

Interesting fact: witches weren't that common in Iceland during the dark years of the Middle Ages. The ones who practiced magic or sorcery were most of the times men. In Icelandic, they're called "Seiðmenn" as "Seiður" was the magic ritual people performed during the Viking Age.

However, I wanted to write about an Icelandic female witch and the things only they can conjure.

One of such things is the creature in this story: a Tilberi.

I didn't specify how the witch created the Tilberi, but here's how you do it: Get a dead man's rib and some wool. Then keep it between your breast and spit sanctified wine from three Sunday communions on it. After three Sundays, it will become alive and in order to feed it, you must let it suck blood from a special nipple that grows on your inner thigh. Then you can make it fetch things for you, such as wool or milk.

Icelandic witchcraft is so gross and fun.

THE YULE LADS ARE COMING

The Yule Lads are as important to the Icelandic society as all the lights we put up when the darkness takes over. To me, and probably most of Icelanders, they herald the actual preparations for Christmas.

Most Icelanders know that the Yule Lads were pranksters back in the day, but with the commercialization of Santa Claus through the Coca-Cola commercials, they became benign and are still used as tools to keep children well-behaved before the Christmas holidays. After all, no child wants a potato in their shoe.

I've loved the stories about the Yule Lads since I was a child and I was particularly fond of their mischievous behavior (at that time, I was a bit of prankster myself – carrying a wooden slingshot and wearing overalls like Dennis the Menace), so for this horror story I wanted to crank up their pranks, to the point that it becomes their very own revenge tale (because I'm a sucker for revenge stories).

I initially wrote the story for Gabino Iglesias's *Halldark Anthology*, but sadly it didn't fit the Hallmark vibes. I hope, however, readers get a kick out of this unusual Christmas story.

THE PERFECT TIME

The Terminator: Judgment Day really fucked me up as a kid; it made me think about the future of our world a whole lot (and probably became the one of the triggers of my anxiety?). What would happen after civilization ended popped into my head often as well as the question how would we survive?

Bunkers are unheard of in Iceland, but they've always fascinated me. How the structure works, and the time people put into them when it comes to resources.

But I've always wondered, what will happen when those resources dwindle? Will the residents leave the bunkers, or will they do the unthinkable to survive a few more years underground?

That's how I came up with the story, but I added in the bond of siblings, which is a staple trope in my stories, but with a twisted twist.

WHAT PROTECTS OUR HERITAGE:

AN ICELANDIC CRYPTID STORY

I love the selfless work the SAR does for people, be it Icelanders or clueless tourists. No matter the weather, the time of day or if they're understaffed, they will still venture out into the harsh Icelandic environment and help those who need it.

Therefore, I wanted to give them a challenge by facing a force of nature they've never encountered before.

Most of Icelandic folklore involve some kind of creature or monster, and they all have an area where they have allegedly been seen. The plane wreckage at Sólheimasandur is, in fact, a popular tourist spot, grown increasingly more popular after Justin Bieber displayed it in one of his music videos. The Icelandic monster called "Skeljaskrímsli", or simply Shell Monster, had been known to dwell in the south of Iceland, so it became the perfect creature for the story.

I named the main character after my father who's an experienced highlands driver. I think he would get a kick out of reading this story, especially since I put his old Nissan Patrol in there as well. He bought the SUV in 2001 and it still fucking works, albeit it's a high possibility you'll get car sick while sitting in it.

I had Ellen Ripley in mind when I created Snædís because she's my absolute favorite female character in horror, but I also thought of the tenacity and independence of Icelandic women. There's a certain word for describing us Icelandic women, "kvenskörungur", which means a very tenacious and hard-working woman, and I think that describes Snædís well.

ACKNOWLEDGEMENTS

It feels surreal that my third short story collection is out now, but I couldn't have made it without the help of these wonderful people.

Steve and Heather at Brigids Gate Press, for believing in my stories and getting them out to the world.

Kev Harrison, for the beautiful introduction.

Stephanie Ellis, for the terrific formatting and shaping my book into the form I'm proud of.

Kristina Osborn, for the kickass cover. The Skeljaskrímsli is so terrifying and the look of the plane wreckage is so ominous.

And you, dear reader, for reading my short stories. I hope you enjoyed them.

About the Author

Villimey has always been fascinated by vampires and horror, ever since she watched Bram Stoker's Dracula when she was a little, curious girl and was traumatized by watching Aliens when she wasn't supposed to. She loves to read and create stories that pop into her head unannounced. Drawing the characters from said stories has always helped with the creative process.

She lives in Iceland with her husband and two cats, Skuggi and RoboCop. When she's not busy sorting through story ideas in her head, she enjoys drawing, reading, playing Dungeons & Dragons or watching the latest shows on almost any streaming site.

Villimey is the author of vampire horror Nocturnal series which currently comprises 4 books; *Nocturnal Blood*, *Nocturnal Farm* and *Nocturnal Salvation, Nocturnal Liberation*. She has released two short story collections called *As the Night Devours Us* and *Visceral Discoveries*. Some of her short stories have been published in various anthologies, including *Slash-Her, Campfire Macabre, The One That Got Away: Women of Horror Anthology Vol. 3, Far From Home, Hex-periments, Were-tales: A Shapeshifter Anthology, Blood in the Soil, Terror on the Wind*.

Twitter: @VillimeyS

Website: www.villimeymistauthor.com

ABOUT THE ARTIST

Kristina Osborn is a graphic artist, indie publisher (Truborn Press) and military veteran based in Washington State with over 15 years of multimedia experience. She specializes in book design, crafting visually engaging layouts that enhance the reader experience. A dedicated mother to a young child, Kristina combines her strong work ethic, discipline, and creativity to deliver impactful designs.

Content Warnings

The Girl with the Hooves
Child abuse
Bullying
Attempted child murder
Graphic death
Human consumption

Survival of the Fittest
Radiation poisoning
Animal death
Child death

They Came From the Rocks
Mutilation
Auditory and visual hallucinations
Graphic death

Hell of a Ride
Child death

The Perfect Time
Implied incest
Implied cannibalism

The Yule Lads Are Coming
Animal death
Torture
Graphic death

Tupperware Party
Penis removal
Dismemberment
Graphic deaths

The Hag's Gift
Mentions of rats
Breastfeeding gone wrong

All-You-Can-Drink Buffet
Workplace bullying
insect bites

What Protects Our Heritage
Mentions of misogyny
Graphic deaths
Animal/creature death
body desecration

MORE FROM BRIGIDS GATE PRESS

THEY HIDE

Francesca Marie

Who are we if not for the monsters that we keep?

They Hide: Short Stories to Tell in the Dark collects thirteen chilling tales that weave through the shadows, exploring the nature of fear, powerlessness, and control.

- A series of murders in a New England colony
- An untamed beast in pre-revolutionary France
- A mysterious stranger who invades 18th-century Ireland
- A traveling circus that takes more than the price of admission
- A gathering of the Dark, telling tales on the longest night of the year, and more.

Come play with vampires, werewolves, ghosts, zombies, ghouls and the devil himself. Make sure you check under the bed and don't turn out the light.

LOVE THE SINNER

Mo Moshaty

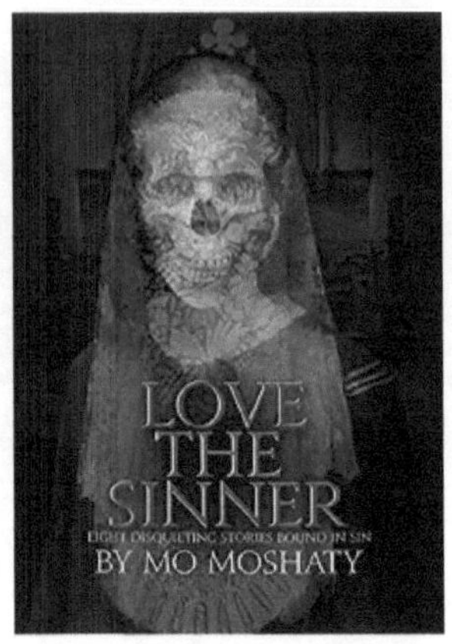

According to Dante, a sin is the misdirection of love - the human will, or essentially, the direction of our beings. *Love the Sinner* is an examination of just how those sins can kaleidoscope into horrific consequences creating a distorted and deadly landscape. These stories stand stark before you in full glaring misstep and macabre to show the human psyche in all its twisted reality.

From grief and its rage to medical meddling to ensure a new world order to bloody revenge within a quantum leap, these stories seek to solidify one absolute truth: man is the scariest monster.

THROWING SHADOWS

Jerry Roth

A woman develops an unhealthy obsession with a scarecrow. A boy plays with a Ouija board and receives a terrifying warning of murder. A down-on-his-luck father learns what happens when you die in your sleep. These stories and six more frightening tales await the reader within the pages of *Throwing Shadows: A Dark Collection*.

Throwing Shadows will feed that hungry dark side that lives in your cellar.

EXTINCTION HYMNS

Eric Raglin

A vengeful owl haunts the man who poached her. A desperate entrepreneur holds a ghost hostage for profit. An addict finds hope and terror in an imprisoned angel. A father and son search their dying world for something to eat other than human flesh. Eric Raglin, author of *Nightmare Yearnings*, returns with his second collection of horror and weird fiction. Strange, terrifying, and tender, these eighteen stories explore what happens when extinction comes for us all.

Visit our website at: www.brigidsgatepress.com